Readers R

Yumi
Talks the Talk

Tea Emesse

MIRROR
STONE

YUMI TALKS THE TALK

©2006 Wizards of the Coast, Inc.

All characters in this book are fictitious. Any resemblance to actual persons, living or dead, is purely coincidental.

This book is protected under the copyright laws of the United States of America. Any reproduction or unauthorized use of the material or artwork contained herein is prohibited without the express written permission of Wizards of the Coast, Inc.

Published by Wizards of the Coast, Inc. STAR SISTERZ, WIZARDS OF THE COAST, MIRRORSTONE, and their respective logos are trademarks of Wizards of the Coast, Inc., in the U.S.A. and other countries.

Printed in the U.S.A.

The sale of this book without its cover has not been authorized by the publisher. If you purchased this book without a cover, you should be aware that neither the author nor the publisher has received payment for this "stripped book."

Cover art by Taia Morley
Interior art by A. Friend
First Printing: April 2006
Library of Congress Catalog Card Number: 2005928123

9 8 7 6 5 4 3 2 1

ISBN-10: 0-7869-3992-3
ISBN-13: 978-0-7869-3992-3
620-95474740-001-EN

U.S., CANADA,
ASIA, PACIFIC, & LATIN AMERICA
Wizards of the Coast, Inc.
P.O. Box 707
Renton, WA 98057-0707
+1-800-324-6496

EUROPEAN HEADQUARTERS
Hasbro UK Ltd
Caswell Way
Newport, Gwent NP9 0YH
GREAT BRITAIN
Please keep this address for your records

Visit our website at www.mirrorstonebooks.com

In loving memory of my niece, Zoe
Chastain-Shannon, who adored animals
and art—and whose beauty, kindness, and
spirit will never be forgotten. And with love
to those adorable Warner girls: Gabriella,
Flannery, Leia, and Victoria.

Chapter 1

People say I'm a drama queen, but I swear I'm not exaggerating when I say my life was perfect until the day I met a monster and had to bring it home. That Saturday, my entire life changed in a shocking way.

But, hey, I'm getting way ahead of myself.

Like I said, it was a Saturday. In the Suzuki household, that means sleeping in. At around noon, Dad cooked us French toast. We all ate leisurely, passing sections of the newspaper back and forth across our gleaming black table.

I started the crossword puzzle—in ink, of course. The three of us participated, with me shouting out clues:

"A four-letter word for 'merely'!"

"Just!" Mom snapped back.

When I crowed, "It's finished—and perfect!" my folks gazed at me dotingly.

"That's our girl!" Dad said.

Mom ate another nibble of French toast, and stretched. "Ah, weekends!" she said. "The very best time to hang with the people you love."

Then we all smiled at each other.

Let's just get one thing straight. I like my parents.

The three of us rinsed dishes and stuck them in our stainless steel, no-noise dishwasher—ultra-modern like everything else in the Suzuki house.

"Ready to hit it?" I asked Mom. "Those garage sales are waiting for us!"

"I'm almost done here," she said, wiping down counters.

"Good. I'll grab your garage sale coat."

Garage sales are the best. This is where Mom and I pick up the goodies we make into curious art and artistic curiosities. Our art projects are quite excellent, or at least "interesting." Okay, that may not sound modest, but it *is* true. Sometimes I wear my art; other times I hang it on the wall or from the ceiling or put it on the floor, to be admired.

I fished through our overflowing "junk" closet in our state-of-the-art home theater room. Ah! Got it!

"Come and get it!" I called. "One coat perfect for picking through other people's trash and treasures!" And it was, according to Mom Suzuki's Scientific Method of Garage Sale Dressing. It was the perfect grayish-brown, all the better not to show smudges. The coat had enormous pockets, in which Mom stashed tape measures (to be sure potential furniture purchases would fit in our house), candy bars (to keep our energy up), cash (since most garage sales won't deal with plastic), a list of sizes (all the better to outfit people with), and so on.

I headed toward the hall, stopping to admire my own reflection in the mirrored closet door. I had thrown on my in-your-face-and-loving-it ensemble, a mint green 1940s-style cotton housedress (think Auntie Em in *The Wizard of Oz*) over a red lumberjack long-underwear shirt. I accessorized with a pair of big black hiking boots and a sparkly barrette holding one lone short ponytail. ("Grow, hair! Grow!")

I looked quite cool, if I say so myself, and I had assembled my outfit in just five minutes, unlike Mom who was still puttering around in slow motion looking for her shoes.

Ho hum. I ambled slowly through the hall toward my bedroom, past all the framed artwork—from my very first dabble-in-finger-paints efforts clear up to my most recent collage composed only of labels cut from our clothes.

Wham! As always, my senses tingled when I walked through my doorway. The jungle mural covering my walls still shocked me every time with its contrast to the minimalist modern theme in the rest of the house.

I'm not a patient waiter (or even a waitress—heh heh. Get it?). I turned on my computer to check my email, since Mom was taking so-o-o-o long.

Oh, good! At least I had an email from my cousin Deb in California, aka "California Cuz." I was reading about this crush Deb had on a guy who was teaching her to surf when I heard Mom's footsteps in the hall. Mom wasn't usually this slow. It was like she had molasses on the bottoms of her slippers, sticking her to the floor with every step, or something. Very strange.

But things were about to get much stranger.

"Mom!" I said, typing a quick note to Deb. "Are we going to hit the road? All the good stuff is going to be . . ."

I heard Mom running down the hall to the bathroom.

✲ ✺ ✲

That's right. Running. I've never seen Mom run anywhere. Like, in my entire life. Yet, there she went, faster than a speeding cougar—okay, faster than a turtle in a big honking hurry.

"Mom?" I called as she slammed the door behind her.

She didn't answer, but I was distracted anyway. I was telling Deb about the dragon lamps Mom and I had just finished making, when all of a sudden a huge—and I mean *huge*—cartoon picture of a cat filled the monitor screen.

"NO!" I screamed. I covered my mouth, all the better to contain my screeches, and backed away from the computer. "*Yuck.* Get out of there."

Dad had put a great pop-up buster on my computer, along with the very best of spam catchers, etc., etc. (My dad knows his computers.) How had this thing gotten through?

I started frantically trying to close it. Sure, the picture of the cat was "cute"— if you happen to like cats.

I did not.

It's not like I was afraid of cats.

Exactly.

Well, maybe somewhat.

Okay, quite a bit.

Yes, actually, I was terrified of cats. In fact, just looking at this cat cartoon was giving me a case of the heebie-jeebies. And, no matter how hard I tried, I couldn't seem to close it.

"Dad?" I yelled, in the general direction of the kitchen, where he was no doubt drinking espresso and reading those fascinating (this is sarcasm, people!) computer magazines of his.

Man. This better not be an omen for the day.

Just as I managed to close the dreadful kitty pop-up, a computer error message appeared: "Click link for more information." Oh, great. Now what had I done? Dad was going to kill me if I imploded yet another computer. Even worse, he might go for the excruciating "teachable moment" routine where he'd spend an hour explaining where I'd gone wrong—an explanation I would understand zilch of.

He can't seem to believe that I'm not as into computers as he is. He jokes that I'm rebelling when I am sometimes the tiniest bit computer clueless. But, the thing is, I have no interest beyond the necessities (like emailing and IM-ing friends, and reading art zines. And, oh, right—doing homework.) It's hard to work up expertise in something that bores you.

I listened. Silence. Mom was still in the bathroom.

Dad was probably deep in the latest technological advances.

Okay. Maybe I should try to fix it for myself . . .

Like I said, I can't wait for things.

I clicked on the link and read the message that popped up.

HUH????

I read it again.

Then I read it out loud:

ATTENTION: Talk to an animal in its own language.

I took my glasses off. I rubbed my eyes. I got out my special glasses cleaner and my special glasses cleaner cloth (the ones I almost never bother to use). I scrubbed my lenses to within an inch of their lives, and I even dusted off the rhinestones on the winged frames. I looked again.

ATTENTION: Talk to an animal in its own language.

Was this some kind of computerese that everyone else in the computer-literate world understood? As I watched, the error message shrank slowly down to the size of a fingernail, and then it said, "Poof!" (I mean,

I actually heard a little poof sound, the way you do during a cartoon when something vanishes). It disappeared, only to show the cartoon cat picture again, which also shrank down, poofed, and departed.

I walked to the door, stuck my head in the hall, and hollered, "DAD!! I NEED YOUR HELP WITH MY COMPUTER."

Nothing. And usually Dad would come instantly to help his darling daughter with anything, but especially the computer. Which he could then try to teach me about so I could (in his words) "discover the beauty inherent in CPUs."

I tiptoed down the hall. Strange. The bathroom door was closed and I could hear water running, Mom splashing away, and whispering. My mom was in the bathroom. Still. Now it appeared from the murmuring that my dad was in there, also.

They seemed to be having the kind of parental whispered conference that only some quite outrageous behavior on my part brings on. I mean "outrageous" in the "Yumi invited everyone in her eighth-grade class over for a party without asking her parents" sense—not "outrageous" in a "Yumi said she will always hate computers" sense. (I must say here, that even when I actually did invite thirty eighth-graders over, my mom rallied like crazy. She gave us all popcorn and lemonade, made up some party games on the spot, had us make art out of trash, played loud music so we could dance, and we all had a spectacular time.)

But this time, I hadn't done anything that warranted a big whispered bathroom confab. For roughly half a second, I considered the fact that it might actually not be me they were whispering about.

Nah, I was the center of their lives—and rightfully so. What else in the world would they have to discuss? What was going on?

I waited a minute. I didn't exactly press my ear to the door, but I was tuned in for anything interesting in their whispering. Couldn't they speak up?

Mom whispered urgently, "Couldn't be," then lowered her voice back to whisper, whisper, whisper.

Oh, brother.

I pounded on the door. "Dad! I need you! Like, seriously."

There was a silence. Then, "Okay, Yumi, I'll be there in a second."

The door opened and he stepped out. When Dad says "a second," that's what he means. Evidently.

"What is it?" he asked.

"Some weird computer message. It's gone, though."

He stared at me. "Well, what did it say?"

"Something about talking to an animal in its own language?"

"Must be an ad of some kind." Dad shrugged.

"Computer woes, yet again?" Mom was chuckling, but she sounded . . . different. Kind of weak. Or shocked, or something. She looked pale, too, even though she'd obviously swiped a little blusher on her cheeks in an effort to banish the "I've just seen a ghost and I didn't enjoy the experience" look. She leaned in the bathroom doorway like she'd fall down without the support.

I felt a little creeped out when I saw her looking like that. I mean, Mom was so incredibly healthy. She could out-shop me any day, and I'm a marathon shopper.

I grabbed her and hugged her. "Mom? Are you okay?"

"Oh, sure she is!" Dad said in a weirdly hearty voice. (My dad is not a hearty-voiced kind of a guy.)

"You look pale," I said to Mom.

"To tell you the truth, Yumi," Dad said, "I think your mom just feels exhausted."

Mom nodded and closed her eyes. I let go of her, and she sagged for a minute before propping herself back up.

Exhausted? My high-energy, never-stops-going mother? I was speechless, for once in my life.

"You're going back to bed." Dad grabbed Mom's elbow like she was ninety years old and turned her toward their room.

"No," Mom said. "I'm okay to go. Where's my garage sale coat, Yu?"

"No," Dad said. "There is no reason for you to go out not feeling well. You and Yumi can go scrounging through other people's junk next weekend. You need a nap."

"I hate to admit it, but your dad has a point." Mom yawned loudly. "Sorry about the garage saling and lunch, girlfriend. Maybe we'll hit it later?"

I just stared at her shuffling down the hall, led by Dad.

"Maybe I'm getting the flu or something," Mom mumbled.

I followed them down the hall and watched Mom kick off her shoes.

She sat down on the edge of their bed like her legs would no longer hold her up. She yawned twice. Poor Mom! I couldn't believe it. She was the one who never, ever got sick even when Dad and I were sniffling (or worse).

I put my arm around her shoulders. "You just rest. Want me to bring you some ginger ale or something?"

Mom hoisted herself up against the pillows slowly and with great effort, kind of like she had cement in her underwear. "No, thanks, honey. I just want to sleep."

I stood there a moment, hoping she'd suddenly feel better.

She opened her eyes. "What's that famous garage band rocker, Nova Darling, doing today? Why don't you two head to the mall?" And her eyelids snapped shut. She began to snore almost instantly.

"Here you go, honey," Dad whispered, handing me a twenty. "Treat Nova to a smoothie or a mocha or something."

Typical. It's not like my folks have tons of bucks or anything, but they always seem to have a little extra for me.

"Can I get you and Mom something? Do you think Mom would want a Mango Tango smoothie?"

Mom opened her eyes. She swallowed hard. She put her hand on her forehead. "Honey, that's sweet of you. But no thanks. Not today."

Mom must be truly sick if she was turning down Mango Tango. Yikes. It boggled my mind.

I backed out of Mom's room, then stood outside her door for a bit.

Suddenly, I was remembering all the motherless kids I'd ever seen in movies or read about. Like Harry Potter, Annie, the Boxcar kids, Nancy Drew, Bud from *Bud, Not Buddy.* I burst into tears.

I should go tend to my mother! I could be her nurse, and coax her gently back to health. Yes, I could see it now. I wiped my eyes on the hem of my skirt and stepped through the door.

Mom snored, oblivious to my healing intentions.

Dad scowled and jerked his hand toward the door. "Go on," he mouthed soundlessly.

And so I did.

Chapter 2

Nova's hair looked even wilder than usual after we biked over to the mall. She went way beyond helmet head. In fact, the helmet didn't seem to flatten out her hair as much as it did for yours truly. As soon as she took her helmet off, her hair sprang forth in all its red and wavy glory. Hey, I'd be overwhelmed with delight to have hair like Nova's instead of my subdued and dull black bob (which I'm growing out!). Nova, however, has a different opinion of her tresses.

"Yeesh," she said. She stroked her head, trying to tame her curls. It was of no use. "Don't even tell me what this bird's nest looks like," she said, finally.

"Nova!" I said, for like the gazillionth time. "I love your hair! It has such presence!"

"Yeah. Right. Whatever," she said, for like the gazil-lionth time.

I whipped a couple of sparkly clips out of my pocket. "Want me to fix you up a bit? Although you look fine."

Nova stood still, ducking down a bit, since I'm a bit height-challenged compared to her. A few seconds of twisting and pinning . . .

"There," I announced. "You look like you belong on the cover of a magazine!"

"Yeah. Like 'Frizz-Buster's Weekly'!" She patted her subdued head.

You know, I suspect Nova likes her hair a lot more than she claims to. Otherwise, she would have chopped it off and/or straightened it a long time ago. But, shhhhh, we won't let on that we're on to her. Let's just keep it our little secret, shall we?

"Oh, look," Nova squealed. She pointed at a couple of little kids crouched over a cardboard box.

Nova grabbed my hand and pulled me toward them.

Uh-oh. I had a bad feeling about this.

"Nova, wait," I said. I laughed a little bit—hoping I sounded light and merry instead of frantic and hysterical. "It's probably just puppies or kittens or something. Let's not go look at them."

Nova pulled me onward like she was a magnet irresistibly attracted to a refrigerator door. She didn't even seem to notice that I had my brakes on and was skidding along beside her. That girl doesn't know her own strength. Although she is no longer taking ballet lessons, she's all muscle from all those years of dancing.

"We can't take an animal home, anyway." As I continued to protest, Nova continued to ignore me and pull me ever closer to the kids and their box.

Please don't be anything that slithers around and meows.

"Maybe I'll just go. I can meet you inside," I said feebly. We were already standing at the box. Like a nightmare you can't awaken from, I saw the sign, which read FREE KITTENS.

"Hi," a woman called from a nearby beat-up junk-mobile. "Those cute kitties have all had their shots! We can't keep them."

Yeah. WhatEVER, lady. Don't tell me your problems.

Nova waved at her. "We're only looking," she said.

You may be looking. I'm not looking.

"Go ahead and pick one up," Ms. Gotta-Get-Rid-of-the-Kittens screeched.

Nova gracefully swooped down.

"No thanks," I said. "Please no. Thanks anyway. I think I'm allergic."

But it was too late. Nova had plopped a fluffy orange ball on my chest. She had a glossy black little monster in her arms, and she was cooing at it like it was her very own human baby. Oh, brother.

Instantly, a million of my sweat glands began to produce perspiration, which ran in rivers over my entire body. (Overdramatic, you're saying? You're wrong! I'm telling you the truth.) I stared fixedly at Nova. Rescue me! But my best friend (who never would have dreamed that her totally confident buddy was actually terrified of felines) whispered down at the creature in her hand, "Are you just a little puddy-tat? Huh?" like some kind of demented cartoon character.

I opened my mouth to say, "Nova! Get this animal off me," but my mouth was so dry I couldn't even croak out the first syllable of her name. I tried to swallow, but I had no saliva.

How could I get the kitten off my chest without actually touching it? I glanced down. The kitten was looking at me. I panicked. I looked around blindly, trying to pretend to myself that I was just standing there without another life form clinging to my person.

An electronic sign flashing in the entry of the mall caught my eye. I focused on it. It read:

ATTENTION: Talk to an animal in its own language.

HUH?

Wait a minute. Wait just one tiny second here. Wasn't that the exact same message I'd gotten on a computer that very morning?

Oh, man. I was absolutely going bonkers!

Hey, I was never even around animals . . .

Oh.

I looked down at my chest. The baby cat looked back at me.

Right.

I cleared my throat.

I looked around. Everyone was watching Nova, who was now actually singing a lullaby to her little bundle of shiny black fur. Was she crazy? (Or was I?) People don't actually sing to animals, right? They don't talk to animals, that's for sure. At least I didn't.

I wasn't really going to do this, was I?

I stared at the sign, still flashing its weirdo message.

I guess I was.

"Uh," I whispered down in the general direction of

my chest. "Meow?" Of course, I felt like the biggest fool in the entire universe. Talk about lame.

I looked up. No one was paying attention to me, thanks to Nova, who appeared to be waltzing with her kitten. I couldn't take that girl anywhere . . . at least anywhere around a cat, evidently.

"Meow?"

Startled, I looked down at that kitten on my chest that had (I swear!) just asked me a question.

"What?" I said.

And then something happened. Something amazing. Something stunning. Something simply shocking.

Little Icky Disgusting Fluff Ball started to vibrate.

"Are you purring?" I asked.

She blinked at me slowly.

"Meow, mrrrr-ow, mew-mew?" I said. (Which actually translates into "I still don't like you because I don't like cats.")

Sure, it was cool it was purring. But still . . . cats were creepy. With a capital C.

It rubbed its face against my thumb. Then, it did it again. It purred louder, sounding like a motorcycle engine. It was hard to believe such a big sound could come out of such a small creature.

"All right, already," I grumped. "Someone get this thing off my chest, okay?"

"A lady took the one I was holding," Nova said. Her voice startled me.

I wheeled around. "Let's give this one back to the . . ." I stopped in dismay. The FREE KITTENS box, along with the kids, was gone. "What the . . . ?"

"They must be in their car," Nova said. "Or shopping."

"Why would they go away like that?" I screeched, scanning the parking lot. "Their car isn't here, Nova! They've escaped!"

We stared at each other.

"They wouldn't," Nova said.

"Oh, no? Oh, no? They just did. They dumped it on me and left!" I stared at the animal. It looked like a rat with long orange hair. I shuddered. "Nova!" I gasped. "What are we going to do?"

Nova stared at the rat—I mean, "cat"—clinging onto my chest. "She's yours, Yumi."

"What?" I stuck the creature on Nova's shoulder. "No, it is not. It almost matches your hair, anyway."

"Sorry," she said, and shoved it back. "I can't take her. Mom's allergic, so no can do."

"No can do, here, too!"

"Yumi," Nova said. "Do you want little Fluffo here to go to the pound?"

"The pound? No! Of course not!"

"Well, then . . ."

Oh, man. I stared at Nova pleadingly. "Please, Nova?"

She spread her hands and shrugged. "I just can't." She leaned over and kind of kissed at the little monster in my arms. "Besides, your mom really likes animals."

A sense of helplessness filled me. "Okay. I guess I'll take it home . . ."

Nova started dancing up and down.

"But only until I can find someone else to take it."

Chapter 3

Nova and I were soon walking our bikes home. I'd stuck the little monster in my bike basket so I wouldn't have to keep touching it. Ugh. I was sure I could smell cat fur on my hands . . . probably all over me. I needed a shower, stat.

"So," Nova said. "What are you going to name her? Fluffo seems about right." She looked at the bundle of orange fur. "Or, hmm. How about Punkin Kitty? That's cute."

"I'm not naming it," I said. I looked away from the orange monster. It seemed to be staring at me. "Remember? I'm not keeping it."

"Still. You've got to call her something."

I shrugged. "Not necessarily."

"Yumi! I can't believe it. You're being so harsh."

"Yeah, well, I'd like to name it 'This thing's got to go' because it does!"

"Togo? Cute!" Nova pursed her lips and looked dreamy. "Yep. That's got class. Togo."

"Nova! I'm not naming it. There's no sense in getting attached."

When we got to the corner where Nova and I always meet and leave each other, halfway between our homes, she lingered, scratching the creature in the basket under its chin and behind its ears. The cat closed its eyes in ecstasy.

Dis*gusting*.

"Are you sure you can't take it home?" I asked.

Nova sighed. "I told you. I can't. My mom is allergic. I can't believe you'd be so mean toward a helpless animal." Nova rolled her eyes and waved her hand. "Whatever. Later."

"Wait!"

Nova stopped. We looked at each other.

"Well, I should have told you before, I guess. It just didn't come up. But I detest cats."

Nova's eyes bugged. "Huh? I had no idea. But why?"

I shrugged.

"Well." Nova frowned at the cat, and then petted

it. "Maybe you'll get over it. Maybe you'll want to keep her."

"Don't count on it."

Nova bit her lip. "I had no idea or I wouldn't have insisted you take her. I apologize."

I felt so close to Nova, closer even than usual. I could tell her anything, I knew.

"Okay," I said. "I'm going to tell you something else. You're going to think I'm crazy. A totally bizarre thing happened earlier today. Actually, I got this weird message . . ."

I bit my lip. Even just saying that much made me sound pretty loony-tunes, frankly. Even a great friend like Nova, who was sensitive and caring, was going to have a hard time with me seeing messages all over the place. Maybe I shouldn't tell this story, after all.

I looked at Nova, who was standing as still as a statue, her eyes fixed on me like tiny green Martians had appeared and were French-braiding my eyebrows.

"Message . . .?" she said in a wispy voice.

"Never mind," I said. I started wheeling my bike along. "I'm going home."

But Nova didn't move. She just stood there, staring. Then she said something amazing.

"You got a message . . . too?"

Too?

I wheeled around to face her. "What do you mean, 'too'?"

She bit her lip.

"Nova? You've gotten messages?"

She nodded, slowly. "What did yours say?" she asked. "And where did you see it? Tell me, tell all!" She started jumping up and down.

"Nova? You're making me worry about you."

She laughed. "Tell me about your message! Then I'll tell you about mine!"

"Well . . . okay. I guess." I told her the whole thing, about the computer cartoon cat and the computer error message and what it said. And then how the sign at the mall said the very same thing. And how I meowed at the cat and it meowed back and started purring.

"But don't think I was enjoying any of it! I was only doing it because I was scared to death and I didn't know what else to do." I sighed. "If I hadn't done it, though, I'd have been paying more attention. The people trying to ditch their kittens wouldn't have gotten away. Now I have to take this thing home and it was all due to the weird messages," I said. "So, tell me! Did you get a message on your computer?"

"Not on my computer, but I've gotten two messages," Nova said. She jumped up and down some more, and hugged me.

I just kind of stood there, blinking at her. This was all going too fast for me.

"My first message was on an ATM screen. You know, they usually say, 'Thanks for banking with us,' or whatever. But this one said, 'Act like a rock star in front of a group of strangers.' I was like "HUH?" but eventually I *did* act like a rock star . . . remember?"

"Story hour!" I exclaimed, remembering Nova singing to a group of little kids. She really hammed it up, too. They loved it.

"It changed my life, as you know." She looked at her charm bracelet. "And then, there are the charms. They're kind of a reward, or something."

"Charms? Really?" I said. "Why didn't you tell me?"

"Oh, Yumi! I've wanted to, so many times! But it just sounded so incredibly . . . out there! I mean, how could I explain something I couldn't even explain to myself? And, besides—I just wanted to kind of hug it to myself, keep it close and personal. But I always knew I'd tell you about it sooner or later."

"Tell me more!"

Nova said slowly, "You know, I don't think I'm going to tell you any more. Because it would take some of the fun out of it all if I blabbed all about my experiences! I've told you enough, for now. Maybe later on we can talk about it."

"But . . ." I said. "Nova . . ."

Nova shook her head and pantomimed zipping her lips closed. Then she started laughing. "But don't you see? Don't you get it?"

"Get what?"

"Your message! And Togo! It's a sign."

Uh-oh. I wasn't liking this one little bit. "A sign?"

Nova nodded. "I think it all means that Togo is going to be very important in your life."

"Ugh. Why couldn't I get to ham it up in front of a bunch of people?"

"You do that on a regular basis, Ms. Drama Queen! No—it doesn't matter if it's easy for you or not. That's just the way it goes."

Chapter 4

Mom stood in the front door as I rode up. She was just standing there with our shiny black front door flung open like she was breathing the fresh air or something. Weird. Mom is not exactly a fresh air freak. She looked at me as I got off the bike and scooped the cat out of the basket. Holding it as I would hold anything that could turn any second and bite me, sucking my life force (in other words, very far away from my body). I climbed the steps. Mom likes animals, so I was ready for a big "Yumi! You brought me a cat" reaction. However . . .

Shocking News #1: My mom backed away from the creature as if it carried the plague.

"What's *that*?" she said.

"Mom!" I laughed a little bit. Surely she was

putting me on, right? "It's a cat. I got stuck with it. The people who had it took off so I brought it home just until . . ."

Mom didn't laugh. She didn't smile. She said, "No, Yumi."

What? No???

"What do you mean?" I said. I kept on walking into the house. Mom kept on backing up until we were inside the living room, where Dad was drinking coffee and reading computer books, as per usual, BUT . . .

Shocking News #2: My dad was totally ticked off about the cat. In a stunning turn of events, instead of saying, "If you bring it home, darling Yumi, you should have it—anything you want," as I would have bet he'd say, my father actually said, "Why didn't you ask first?"

Excuse me? ASK?

a. I didn't want to ask because I did not want to keep that cat.

b. Since when did I have to ask permission for anything, ever?

"Listen," I said. "What's going on here?"

My parents looked at each other. They looked guilty.

"You're not keeping that cat," Dad said abruptly.

"I don't even want . . ." I started, then stopped. Hey, wait a minute. If I started surrendering over something like this, what next? They'd be thinking they were in charge or something ridiculous like that. That would not do, especially not at my age. Had they decided to start cracking down on me for some reason?

Man.

What a predicament. I did *not* want a cat. Yet I'd have to insist I keep it, on principle.

"I'm fourteen years old, and I'm fully capable of taking care of a kitten," I shouted.

They stared at me.

I forged on ahead. "If I didn't take her, I don't know where she might have ended up." I pointed down at her. She did look (deceptively) vulnerable, innocent, and harmless. "Look at her. Poor little thing."

"This is not a good idea, Yumi," Dad said.

"What? You're going to start denying me stuff now?"

Mom said, "I will *not* clean a litter box."

HUH?

"But Mom!" I said. "You always say, 'An animal in need is a friend indeed!' "

Mom said, "I'm not cleaning a litter box, friend in need or not, indeed." And she said it with a straight face.

"Of course not!" I said.

Oh, ugh. I hadn't even thought about a litter box. How revolting. Puke. "I'm going to clean it. I'll take total care of her. I'll even keep her in my bedroom."

What was I saying? Had I totally lost it?

"You won't even know she's here! Besides, we're saving her life—literally! Can you imagine her . . ." I lowered my voice. "Behind bars at the pound? You know what happens to those strays."

My dad's face softened. "Well . . ."

"Oh, come on," I pleaded. "Besides, I'm not going to keep her forever."

"No?" Dad said.

"No," I said firmly. "Just long enough to find her a good home. I'll ask around at school. We can put an ad in the paper. It's only temporary."

Mom sighed. She still looked pretty pale and tired. I felt bad for making a big scene when she obviously wasn't feeling the greatest. But I still had to stand by my principles, even though I was going to end up having a disgusting, shedding, litter-box-filling roommate.

I'll find it a new home, pronto, I promised myself.

When I looked up, I noticed Mom and Dad looking at each other again . . . like, meaningfully.

Mom shrugged and Dad grinned. I had a hunch my battle was won.

Sure enough, Mom said, "I'm telling you, I'm not going near the litter box. I'm not joking."

"Thank you, Mom!" I think. I made moves to hug her, which was awkward with the hairy rat still curled up in my arms and Mom backing away.

"I don't want cat hair on my robe," she said.

You'd think she was the cat-hater, not me. Whatever. I didn't care. As long as I got to keep the upper hand in this brand new Yumi vs. parents power struggle.

"Iva, honey, why don't you go back to bed and take another little snooze?" Dad said.

"Maybe I will," she said, and stumbled off, yawning.

Dad looked at me. "Do you need anything for . . . uh . . ."

I looked down at the cat. "Nova called her Togo."

"Okay. Need anything for Togo?"

Good old Dad. Sure, it was puzzling that we'd had such a scene over my bringing home a kitten, but he was back! Ready and willing and helpful. Dad and I went down to the local pet store to pick up a litter box, cat food, a cat toy, and a bed.

The whole time Dad and I were shopping, I kept looking for a charm like Nova's. I even thought maybe the pet store would have charms in the shape of animals or something. But I saw nothing.

When we got home, Dad offered to make dinner (which means waffles and bacon or one of his weird stews, since those are about the only things Dad can cook).

But, to my amazement, Mom had actually ordered pizza for dinner. Mom hated pizza. Even weirder: the small pizza Mom ordered for herself had no cheese but was loaded with olives, peppers, and anchovies—all ingredients Mom hates.

Could the day get any stranger?

That night as I got ready for bed, I kept getting startled by flashes of something moving in my bedroom. I'd open my mouth to scream. Then I'd remember. Oh, right: the furry rat. Ugh. The sooner I found a home for that thing, the better.

Right before I went to sleep, I heard a scrabbling nearby. I kept my eyes shut—all the better to block out the sight of my unwelcome visitor. I dozed off but woke to find a soft weight between my feet. My toes felt so nice and warm. Drowsily, I flipped my bedside light on. A circle of orange fluff started purring from its spot on my feet.

How cute, I thought dreamily. And then I really woke up, shocked that I would think such a thing. And in further amazement that I let Togo continue snuggling as I turned out the light and went back to sleep.

My last thought was, It doesn't mean I like her.

Chapter 5

$\mathcal{A}$ couple of days later, Nova and I were talking on the phone after school when she asked about Togo.

"You've got to help me find a new home for this creature!" I exclaimed. "ASAP! Instantly! Like, yesterday! She's totally driving me nuts!"

I didn't tell Nova that each night Togo slept on top of the covers, right between my feet. Every time I woke up, there she was. After all, that meant nothing in the overall scheme of my hatred for felines. I wasn't going to start liking cats now.

She sighed. "I was thinking maybe you'd start loving her."

"That's completely impossible! I mean, it's totally horrible having her around all the time," I said, trying to ignore the creature rubbing against my ankle. She had pretty eyes. For a monster.

"You can come on over," Nova said. "We'll brainstorm ways to find her a new home."

"Hooray! I'm outta here—away from you!" I exulted to the hair-rat.

She blinked up at me and purred loud enough for me to hear.

I made sure she had fresh water, yet again, and a dish of kitty food. I cracked the window for fresh air. Then (speaking of needing fresh air) I held my nose and did the litter box cleaning thing. As soon as it was completely fresh and tidy, the little monster got in to mess it up. Do all cats do that? Probably. They're gross.

I tiptoed into Mom's room. She was napping instead of making art in her backyard studio. Usually, she can't stay away from it. She can barely tear herself away to come inside for mundane things like dinner. In fact, since I was a little kid, I have spent quite a bit of my time in her studio watching her work, making my own projects, and helping her take some of our art pieces into galleries where they actually sometimes are sold.

Mom didn't stir until I said, "Mom? Uh. How are you doing?" Then she stuck her head out of the covers and blinked at me blearily. I repeated my question.

She stuck her head under the covers and said something that came out muffled. It sounded like, "I'm tired of this."

"Well, I guess everyone gets sick on occasion," I said. "Even super-healthy folks like you."

She propped herself up. "What are you up to, Yu?"

"Nova invited me over, but maybe I should stay home and nurse you back to health!" I put my hand on her forehead.

Mom laughed. "I'm okay, Florence Nightingale. Go hang out with Nova."

I biked over to Nova's, where her mother bustled around the kitchen making us good-for-you snacks (sunflower seeds and organic fruit she'd dried herself). Nova rolled her eyes in humiliation.

"Hey, girls, I'm going to run and jump into my leotard," she said, giving the kitchen floor a quick hard sweeping.

"Have a good lesson, Mom," Nova said.

"I always do!" Ms. Darling said, dashing toward her room.

Nova's mom is a total ballet nut. As we headed for Nova's room, I thought about how much happier

Nova was than when I'd first met her. She was taking ballet herself then, and having to practice all of the time. At the same time, she realized her heart was so NOT in dance. She was just dying to play guitar. And now—ta da!—she not only played guitar, but she was in a garage band! And her mom, the one who truly loved being a ballerina, was doing the dance thing.

"Your mom cracks me up," I told Nova as she picked up her guitar, which is this cool old electric guitar called a Stratocaster. It's even got a name—Roxie.

"Tell me about it," Nova said, strumming so fast her fingers blurred. "We're a lot closer now than we used to be when I resented having ballet crammed down my throat. Oh, that reminds me! Have you gotten a charm yet?"

It took me a minute. Oh. The weird message. The phantom charm.

"Nope." I shrugged. "Haven't even thought about it, to tell you the truth. I've been too worried about getting rid of that horrid creature shedding all over my bedroom. It's really nasty."

Nova quit strumming. "So you're really not in love with little Togo?"

"Give me a break. No way."

"Huh. What have you done to find her a home?"

Nova frowned. "Newspaper ads . . . ?"

Okay, so maybe I could have done some of those things—taken out some ads. Why exactly hadn't I? Quickly I went on the offensive, all the better to avoid being defensive.

"You were the one to get me into this mess!" I said accusingly. "All that 'poor little thing, she'll go to the pound' stuff!"

"It was true!"

I crossed my arms over my chest. "Well, you can help me get rid of her."

"Oh, Yumi." Nova set Roxie down. "Sure. We'll think of something. Someone out there is just dying to have a fluffy little orange kitten like Togo in their lives."

I'm not feeling a twinge. I'm not.

"You bet," I said heartily. "Let's brainstorm."

"Obviously, we'll call the local radio station. They've got some kind of pet hour, where they announce lost and found animals, and ones needing homes. And, you can put an ad in the newspaper."

"I don't know. Calling in the media? Doesn't this seem pretty drastic?"

Nova frowned at me. "You want to find a new home for her, right?"

Uh . . .

Wait a minute. Why am I hesitating? I want to get rid of that cat. Seriously. I do.

"Of course!" I said loudly.

Nova kept frowning at me. "Are you sure?"

"Yes!"

"Okay, then. Hmm. We should take pictures and posters around to put on grocery store bulletin boards. Yumi, have you placed an ad on any boards on the Internet?"

Frankly, I think Nova is a little obsessed with the Internet. It's because her parents won't let a computer into their house. I think they're afraid of bad magnetic waves or something.

"I didn't think of it," I told her. "Would that even help? You know there's tons of garbage on the Internet—stuff that looks official, even."

"I know that!" Nova said, like the expert she wasn't. "But how about Craig's List, or something like that?"

"Huh," I said. "I guess that makes sense. I'll do it when I get home."

"Let's bike on down to the Mall-o-Rama library," Nova said. "We can tell everyone there hi, and use their computer."

"Oh, Nova . . . I don't know."

"Come on! Let's do it. I've got a band get-together this afternoon, so if we're going, the time is now."

As we rode our bikes to the library, Nova kept look-ing into my empty basket.

"What?" I said, finally.

"Oh, nothing," she said, in a way that let me know perfectly well it was not "nothing."

"Nova?"

"I just keep remembering how cute that little Togo looked riding in your basket." Nova sighed. "She looked so at home."

I glared at her, trying my best not to picture that little ball of orange fluff. She had looked kind of cute. For a monster. Somehow, though, that image of the unwanted hitch-hiker persisted. Think of something else.

But, you know how it is—the more you try not to think of something, the more you think of it.

When we finally got to the library, the first person we saw was that extremely cool librarian, Blue. She was up on a ladder taping a "KIDS READING PROGRAM" banner across the entry. Her long, tawny hair swooped down the back of her brightly embroidered muslin shirt.

Nova and I said, in unison, "Blue!" and when she turned her head, long silvery handmade-looking earrings glimmered against her freckled cheeks.

"You guys!" she said, beaming. "Are you back to volunteer? I hope?" She climbed down the ladder and stood between us. Even in her extremely high platform sandals, Blue is even shorter than I am. And, believe me, Blue makes "short" look wonderful.

"Sorry," I said.

Nova said, "We'd love to come back, but with school and everything . . ."

"I understand," Blue said. "I'm just full of wishful thinking. I enjoyed you girls so much, and wanted to get to know you better."

"Ditto!" I said while Nova nodded vigorously.

Nova said, "We're here this time to use a computer. Yumi needs to . . ."

Oh, no. Don't say it. Even as I was wishing Nova wouldn't bring up why we were using the computer, I had to wonder what my objection was. Did I just want to make a great impression on Blue—and thought my extreme haste to get rid of an animal might not be the coolest? Probably.

I turned back just in time to hear Nova finish up. "We'll put an ad on some websites. I only wish I could take her. She's so cute."

"I volunteer at the Humane Society," Blue said. "Maybe I can help you out if you don't find another home for her." She stopped and smiled. "I'm tempted to take her myself, just on your description! If I didn't have my big tom cat, Jake, I'd go for it in an instant. He can be pretty territorial . . . he's got this funny, feisty personality. Still, consider me a last resort if you can't find another spot for her. Jake will just have to adjust."

It was plain from the way she spoke that Blue loved animals. Not that she was looking down her nose at me. But I had a hunch Blue would never give away a little kitten.

"Thanks, Blue." Suddenly I felt sad, but I couldn't figure out why.

As we sat down at the computer and Nova started typing in the Craig's List address, a woman near us kept coughing, "Hack, hack, hack!"

"Computer hacker," I whispered to Nova. We swallowed our giggles as the woman rummaged in her purse, then got up and left. There was something about the way she wore her hair that made me think of Mom.

"Cool!" Nova said. "Here's a Middletown classifieds page, and it's free. We'll put an ad here, for sure."

I squelched my annoyance. After all, Nova was just trying to help me—help me be free of that annoying creature in my bedroom.

Distract her, a little voice whispered inside my head.

Just then, the coughing woman came back to her computer station.

"Mom's still sick," I whispered urgently to Nova.

Her red eyebrows rose to meet her hairline. "Huh?"

"Shhh," whispered the cougher.

"Yeah," I murmured in Nova's ear. "Still sick." I made it sound like Mom had the plague instead of a flu bug. I sniffed a little as if I might break down in tears at any minute.

"I'm so worried about her!" I hissed quietly. Man, I was really hamming it up like no one else can. I felt a moment of pride, until I saw how worried Nova looked. I felt bad about manipulating her, but somehow I was becoming utterly weary of this whole "get rid of the cat" quest.

I mean, sure I wanted Togo gone, but did we have to spend all day working on it? Time for a change.

I stared fixedly at the computer, blinking rapidly.

"Oh," Nova whispered. "Maybe we can look up your mom's symptoms and figure out what's wrong with her."

For half a sec, my brain flooded with worry. What if we discovered Mom had some dread disease and was going to die? Right. Quit scaring yourself, Drama Queen.

Nova was muttering quietly to herself: "Queasiness, weakness, tiredness," as she clicked away at the keyboard.

"Does she have a killer headache?"

"I don't think so," I said. "Not that she's mentioned."

"I was thinking migraine," Nova said, like she was a doctor or something. "Hmm . . . carbon monoxide poisoning? Nah, you'd all be sick."

She browsed further.

"Is she coughing?" She said, just as Coughing Woman started hacking away again.

We giggled, trying to smother the noise with our hands.

"No!" I gasped.

"It doesn't sound like anthrax, then."

Anthrax? Oh, brother.

Nova shrugged. "Just trying to rule out diseases."

"You've been watching too much *E. R.*!" I said.

Nova scowled at me. "Remember me? I'm the friend who does not own a television set."

"Oh. Right." I patted her on the back. "Sorry."

"Hmm. Does she have aching joints?"

"Not that I know of."

"Sweatiness?"

I shook my head.

"Breathing problems? Chest pain?"

I kept shaking my head no. Finally, I said, "Nova, let's go, okay?"

"But what about Togo?"

Oh. Right. "Well, we put a few ads on Internet bulletin boards, right? I'll ask my dad to help me put an ad in the newspaper."

"Sounds good. I'm sure you'll find someone who wants her soon. Besides, you've got Blue to fall back on."

I bit my lip.

Nova had to get over to Joe's house to jam with their garage band. To tell you the truth, I was relieved. No offense meant to my best friend, but I was sick of the topic of Togo and her new home/owner. And I felt a little bad for using Mom's flu as a distraction. Time to head home.

Little did I know that what I'd find at home would seriously shake me up.

Chapter 6

Mom wasn't in her studio. Rats. I wanted to get another art project going . . . maybe some jewelry. The house was very quiet.

I went into my room to check my email. As I eased tentatively through the door, I waited for Wretched Kitty to attack my ankles. That had been her latest trick—hiding behind the door and then pouncing on my vulnerable shins, actually chewing on them with her needle-sharp teeth. Who said kittens were cute? They were vicious.

No cat.

Oh-KAY.

Where was she? She wasn't on the bed, under the covers (I don't make my bed except for special occasions), or under the bed. I looked in my closet, and in the pile of clothes that had accumulated on the closet floor. Nothing.

Next I checked behind my dresser and under a pile of papers on my desk. Togo was nowhere to be found.

Okay. So she must have . . . what? I was trying not to panic, but WHERE WAS SHE???? Could she have gotten out of my room? The door was shut when I left, and it was closed when I got home.

Wait a minute.

Wait just one stinking minute.

Why did I even care? I didn't want a cat. Didn't need a cat. Didn't like cats.

I suddenly remembered her soft weight against my feet at night. The way she'd purr so loudly you could hear her anywhere in the room.

I shook my head, hard. What was going on with me?

All I knew was that I wanted to see that little bundle of orange fluff—and I wanted to see her now.

I'll figure it out later. Right now, I'm finding my cat.

My cat????

Whatever.

She had to be in the house somewhere!

I ran down to my parents' room. Maybe Mom let Togo into their room? But Mom wasn't there. I started looking around, behind furniture. Under the bed there were some books, including my baby book. I had a fleeting thought: Aw. Kind of sweet, that Mom was reliving my old baby days.

No kitten, though.

I went into the hall, and then into every room in the house, calling, "Here, kitty, kitty. Here Togo."

She had to be here *somewhere.*

But she wasn't. I looked everywhere.

Mom was stretched out in a lounge chair on the patio next to a big plant with silver-spotted leaves. She had her eyes closed and was cuddled up in her favorite zebra-striped afghan.

"Mom?" I whispered. She didn't even move.

I went inside to call Dad. He was in a meeting. A meeting about computers??? Seriously, what could a group of people even find to say about them? "They're dull. They're boring. Sometimes they don't work."?

I called Nova, but as soon as her answering machine picked up, I remembered that she'd be with her band. I didn't even leave a message. I couldn't trust myself not to cry.

In fact, I *was* crying. I didn't even remember starting, but my face was all wet. I didn't ask myself why.

Because I knew.

The impossible had happened.

I, Yumi Suzuki, hater of all things feline, was in love with a cat!

My beloved kitten was gone. There was no one for me to talk to. I didn't know what to do or where to go.

Chapter 7

I'll fast forward through my big sobbing scene, in which I once again looked everywhere for Togo without finding her. And then got into bed.

I was waiting for Dad, though, when he came in the kitchen, like he always did, at 5:35 sharp. As he always did, he tossed his keys on the counter. Today, though, he had a big and a small pizza box with him.

Pizza, again?

"Your mom's been into it, so . . ." he said, obviously reading the expression on my face.

"Mom hates pizza," I muttered.

I put my arms around Dad. He had this far-away expression on his face. Was he still thinking about his computer meeting?

"Hello?" I said. "I'm here, you know. Your very own daughter."

He chuckled. "I'm aware of that. What's up, honey?"

But when I pulled back to look at him, he again looked like he was far away—like as far away as Mars.

I burst into loud sobbing tears (okay, I guess I earn my "drama queen" description, at least every once in a while). "She's gone!" I bellowed.

Dad's mouth dropped open and he tensed, as if he would run from the room. Yeah!! This is what I'm talking about! A worthy reaction to the dreadful news about my little kitten! Finally!

"Mom?" Dad cried. "Mom's gone?"

"Mom? Of course Mom's not gone!" Sheesh. "Togo! She's absolutely nowhere in this entire house. And I had my bedroom door closed!"

I swallowed. "My window was open just a tiny bit. I wanted her to have fresh air. She couldn't have gotten out, right? Why would she? She loves me!"

Dad's shoulders relaxed and his mouth snapped shut. "Well, honey," he said, in such an offhand voice I wanted to scream, "cats wander sometimes."

"That's it?! Cats wander sometimes? That's how much you care?"

He rubbed his eyes, and then his temples. "Oh,

honey, I'm sure Togo will show up. Besides, you were looking for a new home for her, right?"

"Uh. Yeah. Right."

"So there's no reason for you to be in this much of a state." Dad gave me his well practiced "Calm down, Yumi. Quit being so dramatic" look. "In fact, maybe she went out and found herself that new home."

Yeah. Thanks for caring.

I sniffled. "I think she wanted to be with me. Maybe someone cat-napped her!"

"Oh, please, Yumi." Dad sighed. "The cat will show up when she wants to. No one took her. How's your mom?

Oh, wow. Suddenly, I felt guilty for concentrating so much on Togo while Mom was having trouble shaking her flu.

Dad and I took our slices of pizza out to the patio, carrying Mom's pizza to her on a tray. She woke up with a start.

"Mom? Did you see Togo today?"

"Togo? That cat?"

"Yes, Mom." Gee, thanks for paying attention. "Yes, my cat. She's missing."

"Huh," Mom said. "I imagine she'll show up."

I gnawed on my pizza while my worries gnawed on me. Where was my kitten?

After we ate, the three of us stashed our dishes in the dishwasher.

"I think I'll go read in bed," Mom said.

I followed Dad into his den. He picked up his briefcase and opened it.

I was back to obsessing over Togo. Where was she?

"Maybe I'll call Nova and ask her to come over and study for the history test," I said. Or help me search for my kitten.

Dad looked relieved. "Great idea!" he said with enthusiasm. I guess he was dying to get to his computer, as usual.

Nova was only momentarily stunned when I announced that I now loved Togo, who had gone M.I.A. And, like a true friend, she only said, "I told you you'd love her" once. She and I looked everywhere, even inside the garage and in my parents' cars. But Togo was a no-show.

We finally gave up.

Chapter 8

The next morning, I trudged into the kitchen to find the folks at the breakfast table. I'd had a miserable night. Whenever I'd managed to fall asleep, I would dream Togo was all cuddled up to my feet. When I woke up, I was devastated at how lonely I was without her. I'd definitely have to put up some posters and put an ad in the paper and all that good stuff.

I was a bit appalled to see that Mom was eating pizza for breakfast. Cold pizza. And the pizza was covered with olives and anchovies. Cold slimy olives and cold slimy fishy anchovies. Not exactly your average breakfast of champions. I tried not to shudder.

And I tried even harder not to shudder at what Mom was wearing: some kind of a loose brown linen shift that looked like a paper bag with arm and neck holes in it. What was she thinking? She was an artist, and she dressed like a sack lunch. I looked down at my own "I am an artist" outfit: aqua rayon bowling shirt with the name "Drew" embroidered over the pocket, orange capris, and red cowboy boots with needle-sharp pointed toes. Like nothing anyone else would be wearing today, that's for sure.

Mom, I could fix you up. Fast.

"Hi Mom. Hi Dad." I started fixing myself my favorite breakfast: toast with almond butter. Yum.

"Mom, it's so good to see you back to yourself"—I watched her take a bite of pizza—"for the most part. You're feeling all better?"

My parents looked at each other. They started smiling. Each had a goofy, "I think I've just fallen in love" expression, kind of like something you'd see in a cartoon.

My hair stood on end. Yech. I'm sorry, but:

- Knowing your parents love each other=GOOD.
- Watching them act like giddy teenagers on their first date=VERY BAD.

I cleared my throat and took a bite of toast. "So, Dad, you're glad Mom's on the mend, I guess?"

He took her hand. "I sure am," he said. "Ecstatic."

Okay.

"In fact, I'm so happy, I'm not even going to work today."

Huh? Believe me, my dad does not take time off from work lightly. He loves his company's computer network, and must tend it. Constantly.

"As a matter of fact, I thought it might be nice if you took the day off today and stayed home from school," Dad said.

I dropped my toast and whacked my ear. Somehow, I thought I'd just heard Dad, my father, suggest I PLAY HOOKY!

"Excuse me?"

My weird parents burst out laughing.

I guess I forgot to close my mouth, which had dropped open when Dad said he was staying home, and then fallen completely open when he suggested I do the same. I snapped it shut.

"Why?" Now I was completely alarmed. My parents were acting totally wacky and goofy—not at all like their normal selves.

Naturally, I wanted to stay home from school—what red-blooded teenager wouldn't? Then again, could I stand this giggling and handholding?

"I'll help you make some flyers to find your cat," Dad said.

Oh. Now we were talking.

"Really?"

"And I'll help you get some ads to the newspaper and radio," Mom said. She stood up and kissed the top of Dad's head.

I averted my eyes. Could I take this?

"But first," Dad said, "Mom and I need to tell you something."

Chapter 9

My jaw dropped to my chest. All I could hear was a high-pitched ringing sound. If I was a fainter, believe me—I'd be on the ground.

"Huh?" I said, for the third or fourth time.

And for the third or fourth time, they told me: "You're going to be a big sister!"

"We had a pretty good notion, anyway," Dad said. "From the symptoms and the pregnancy test from the drugstore. The doctor confirmed it yesterday. It's big news! Yep, big news."

"Isn't it a miracle?" my mom cooed. "And here I thought it would never happen."

"A miracle?!" My voice cracked. "You've got to be joking, right?" I looked around for cameras. Were we on one of those crazy reality shows where people played practical jokes and recorded it?

I fell onto the floor, screaming, "This can't be happening! I am going to DIE of embarrassment!!"

"Oh, honey," Mom laughed. "You'll get used to it."

"No, I won't!" I flopped over to my stomach. "I'll never get used to it! You think I'm joking but I'm totally FREAKED OUT!"

I looked up to see how this was affecting my parents. They were smiling these dopey little grins at each other and shrugging. Kind of like, "Oh, that Yumi! Always so dramatic even when she loves the news!"

My head spun. "This is why you've been sick? Morning sickness? And tired, and all that? Are you sure? You're way too old to be pregnant."

Dad, who seemed to have morphed into an all-knowing baby doctor or something said, "Yumi, more women are having babies in their forties all the time. Sometimes even older."

Great. Maybe you can produce an even dozen.

Mom gestured with a piece of pizza. "And I've had all of these weird food cravings!" She giggled, like it was the cutest thing in the world.

Dad sighed, then grinned. "Can you believe I had to go out shopping for rocky road ice cream last night? Or should I say early this morning? It was around two."

Mom patted his hand. "Thanks again, sweetie, from both of us."

Oh, no. Both of us??? Ugh. Please tell me she didn't say that.

My world had officially ended.

"Well," Dad said cheerfully. "What do you think, Big Sis?"

I just stared at him.

"At a loss for words, eh?" Both parents laughed.

I continued to stare up from my position on the floor. That's what shock will do to you. Maybe I'd never get up again.

My (oh, how I hated to even think the word) pregnant mother used the table edge to pull herself up, as if she suddenly weighed a thousand pounds.

"Careful, honey," Dad said, as if she were skydiving instead of standing in her very own kitchen.

She stroked the ugly brown material over her stomach, and I realized she actually had a gut—quite a big one for someone Mom's size!

"You're not going to have to wait too long to meet your baby brother or sister," she said. "I thought I was just putting on a bit of weight, but it turns out I'm quite a bit along in my pregnancy." (I repeat: "my pregnancy." Two words I never expected to hear from my mother's lips, and I flinched at the sound of them.)

Huh. I realized Mom had been wearing a lot of big baggy shirts and tunics lately.

"So, what have we got, Little Mom?" Dad said. "Four months or so to get ready for the new addition to the family?"

"Yep. Not long for all we need to do. I figure we can put the TV in the living room, and fix the TV room up as a nursery . . ."

As my parents rattled on about cribs and paint colors and baby equipment, and telling all the relatives, I couldn't take it any more. I was totally, completely freaked!

I sprang up from the floor, tore out of the room, then out of the house—and kept on running. I pounded along the streets through neighborhoods, not looking to the left. Not looking to the right. Not thinking about Togo. Not thinking about how my entire world had changed and was going to keep on changing because of my parents' news. No. I mind-lessly ran. It felt so good, a true escape—mental and physical.

I was quite a ways from home when I saw Togo. Well, actually, it was a pale orange blur that streaked across the road and down an alley. I flew after her, screaming, "Togo! Togo!" and "Here, kitty, kitty, kitty," until I ran out of breath.

We cut across a few backyards and down another alley. Then across a beautifully green lawn that looked like velvet. Swoosh! Every sprinkler in the entire yard came on drenching me.

My pointy-toed red cowboy boots squished with every step as I chased that cat under a hedge. I was determined, so I slithered under the bushes, gasping out, "Togo? It's me. Come back! I love you now."

I emerged on the other side of the hedge with leaves in my hair, mud on my butt, and sticks in my underpants. (Not really—but it felt like it!)

"May I help you?" a voice said, and then, "Oh! Yumi!"

I couldn't believe my eyes! It was that coolest of all librarians, our very own Blue. She'd smoothed her caramel-colored mane into a French twist. She wore long dangly sparkly earrings and immaculate khaki gardening pants, big red rubber gardening clogs, and a thick white T-shirt. Although she had gardening gloves on and clippers in one hand, she looked like she'd never touched so much as a molecule of dirt.

"Blue!" I said, noticing she was even wearing a

charm bracelet like Nova's, just about the time I noticed she was holding . . .

"Togo!" I gasped.

"Yumi, remember what I told you about my cat, Jake?" Her voice was extra kind, probably because I looked pitiful, all wet and muddy and breathless. "Here he is, in the fur."

Huh?

"I could've sworn . . ."

"I'm sorry, Yumi," Blue said. "Did your cat take off?"

I nodded. "I could swear that's her."

"Him," she said, placing the cat in my arms. And, as soon as I felt his muscular bulk and got a good look at his big square Garfield face, I knew she was right. This wasn't my kitten. It wasn't even a kitten, but a full-grown cat. The power of wishful thinking had led me astray.

"Oh, man. I've been chasing this cat all over the place. And it's not even mine." I blinked at Blue. "But, kind of weird that I'd end up at your house! Sorry for charging through the bushes like that."

"I'd do the same," Blue said. "How long did you say your cat has been missing?"

"Forever . . . or that's the way it feels. Actually, only one day." I blinked hard and stroked Jake. He purred like a motorboat. Funny how I always had feared and distrusted cats. It seemed knowing Togo, even for such a brief period of time, had changed me into a true cat person. My nose got all tingly and I had to sniff a few times. "Blue, I decided not to give up Togo. I love her!" I wailed, "and now she's gone!"

"Jake here takes off for long periods of time," Blue said. "I've actually given up on him a few times, but eventually he comes home. But I know that doesn't help you with your situation. How about a glass of lemonade and some cookies? I made the cookies myself, just this morning. And you could use a towel!"

I hugged Jake closer. "Sounds fabulous! Thanks!"

Blue's home . . . well, it's about what you'd expect from the world's coolest librarian. Her living room held a very low couch covered in brilliant red, purple, and orange hand-woven fabric and a large wooden rocker. Glossy wooden floors, with one huge tree-sized houseplant near the window. A big rock fireplace surrounded by floor to ceiling bookshelves—crammed full of books. (Well, what would you expect?) The room smelled faintly like wood smoke, like she actually used her fireplace in the evenings. Even the towel she handed me was different—enormous, black, and fluffy. It felt so good.

I followed her into her kitchen, where she washed her hands at the sink. Jake wriggled and jumped down to check out his dish.

Blue laughed, "That cat lives to eat. I swear."

Her kitchen was kind of cluttered, but in a good way. There was a big blue bowl of apples on the counter, along with an open cookbook. Racks of cookies lined the counter, and pots of plants grew in the window. The air was fragrant with ginger, molasses, and cinnamon.

"Have a cookie, or ten," Blue said. "I get a little carried away. Want to see the rest of the place before we get out the lemonade?"

"Sure." I took a quick bite of cookie. It was buttery, tender, and spicy. "Yum!"

"Bring it along," Blue said.

I followed Blue into the hall, which was hung with odd, modern-looking, brilliantly colored quilts.

"I made these," she said off-handedly.

"My mom would love to see these. She's an artist, too."

Blue looked as if she'd just won the lottery. "Hey! No one ever calls me an artist! Thanks! Oh, I hope I can see some of your mom's work sometime. I'd love that."

I kind of wanted to say, "I do art, too," but it would

sound like it was such a big deal. It's not like I'm Rembrandt or anything. Still, I take my art seriously.

She led me into her bedroom, which was painted a brilliant, shiny orange with white polka dots. The bedspread was white with big orange polka dots. White and orange throw rugs were scattered on the dark wood floor.

"Whoa!" I blinked at all that brightness.

Blue laughed. "I was in an orange kind of a mood— all happy over my new job here. I believe in making your surroundings reflect your mood."

"What if you get in a deep funk?"

"I'll either hope to ride it out, or I'll paint this room a dark color and turn it into a cave." Blue laughed again. I could tell that she would probably not ever have to live in a dark brown room. Me, on the other hand . . .

"My mom's going to have a baby," I blurted, following her out of her room. "Isn't that, like, the worst news you've ever heard?"

"Oh." Blue quit walking and I ran right into her.

"Sorry!" we both said.

"Let's get that lemonade, shall we?" Blue said.

When we were seated in her living room, sipping and nibbling, Blue said, "Tell me about the new addition to the family."

My throat turned dry. I coughed.

"Goodness," Blue said. "Are you okay? Am I going to have to Heimlich you to clear your airway?"

I hacked a little more. "Nah, I'm all right. Or I would be if my parents weren't so set on destroying my life."

Blue just raised her eyebrows.

"Why would they want another child? Am I not enough for them? Besides, how humiliating to have my mother with a big old belly." I shuddered.

I ranted. I raved. I went on and *on.* Blue just mostly listened sympathetically. She did not give me advice— which was a good thing. She didn't tell me to get over myself, which was another good thing.

She just gave me a little hug and a bag of cookies when I left, along with some promises to get her Humane Society connections in gear to look for my missing-in-action kitty cat.

As I walked home, it hit me how far I'd traveled when I was running away from my parents and their news. Man, I had no idea I could be so fast!

When I got home, I found a note from the folks. They were grocery shopping. They didn't say one word about me taking off. They probably hadn't even noticed I was gone.

I grabbed a Hershey's Special Dark Chocolate candy

bar out of our junk food drawer and went into my room. It was disgustingly cheerful in there. I crawled into my nice dark closet, making a nest in all the shoes on the floor and munched chocolate and Blue's cookies, trying not to think about anything.

It was without a doubt the worst day of my entire life.

A few days after I heard the big, bad news, Dad was passing by my room and stopped in the doorway. I sat on the floor, holding Togo's bed and sobbing. Dad came in. He put his arm around me and said, "Honey, I'll get you another cat."

I yanked away from him. "Another cat? You think another cat will replace Togo?" Sure you do, just like another kid could replace your first one.

He knew I wasn't listening as he apologized. To top off the whole "he just doesn't get it" scene, he brought me an ice cream sundae—like he could buy me off that easily!

Yeah. I don't think so.

"No, thank you," I said frostily.

Then, if you can believe it, he sat down right there and ate my sundae! Right in front of me.

Things went downhill from there, in a hurry.

In the next few days, they started tearing the TV room apart. They moved our huge wide-screen TV to the living room (where it took up half the space, and was hard to watch. You were so close to the actors you were looking up their noses).

Dad, of course, wouldn't let Mom paint: "The fumes! The fumes!" he kept saying. So he took more time off work (being a workaholic, he had plenty of vacation days saved up) because he didn't trust anyone they'd hire to fix his little baby's room the way it should be fixed.

One interminable dinner they spent decades discussing the décor of the new room.

"We're not going to find out whether the baby is a boy or a girl," Dad explained, with all the seriousness of a politician negotiating a peace treaty.

"Like I care," I muttered.

"In fact, tomorrow when we go for Mom's ultrasound, you're going with us, right Yumi?"

"You'd have to drag my dead body."

"Oh, Yumi! You should go and get the first look at your new brother or sister."

I shook my head. "No way."

Mom and Dad looked at each other and sighed simultaneously.

"Well, anyway. We're telling the technician we don't want to know the sex."

"It's more romantic that way," Mom said.

ROMANTIC? There's nothing romantic about any of this.

"You will be at the delivery, though, right Yumi?" Dad asked. (Are you joking???) "We'll all three be surprised by what flavor we end up with."

Gag.

Now, you might be thinking these are all sour grapes from an only child, who's used to being the center of attention.

Well—you would be right. I don't mind admitting it here and now (or there and anytime, for that matter!). I've always proudly been the center of Mom and Dad's universe. Why should that change? Surely they could see, as well, that I am plenty of kid for anyone.

And I didn't like having my life rearranged for some event in the future. So, there was going to be a baby. Big deal. Did we have to lose our cool home theater room? If they were so set on messing up—I mean "adding to"—our family, couldn't they keep the little creature in their own room? Everything in the house was a big mess now, with things pulled out of the TV room, the carpet ripped up, Dad in there painting until all hours of the night (when he wasn't running out for Mom's Ben & Jerry's Chubby Hubby ice cream fix).

And *also*—well, the absolute truth is that I had never liked babies. All they did was spit up on you and cry and make messes in their diapers. Who needed a stinking, crying mess?

Okay. Just one more little thing. No one my age—and I mean no one!!—had a big, waddling, pregnant mom. I mean, it's not only undignified, it's horribly, terribly, unbelievably embarrassing.

Plus, my little kitten was gone. And hadn't shown up. No one had called to report finding her.

My life stunk.

Chapter 10

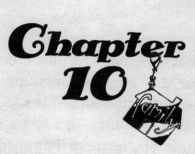

The dreadful days turned into appalling weeks. For once in my life, I was glad to go to school. It was so much better than hanging around Babyville.

Picture this scene from my life: I'm innocently eating breakfast.

Mom says over the pickle and peanut butter sandwich she's enjoying, "Our new baby is so lucky to have such a totally grownup sister!"

"She is getting to be such an adult," Dad says.

I scream, "Give me a break!"

"Yumi," Dad says. "We're complimenting you."

But actually they were panicking me. Were they going to ship me off to boarding school or something? Or maybe find me a job and an apartment? After all, I was a mature fourteen, and ready to live on my own, right?

Wrong.

"I don't think it's the baby so much, do you?" Nova asked me that day after commenting on my total glumness. She closed and locked her locker. "I mean, you'll get used to that idea—it's just a shock at first. Don't you think you're more bummed about Togo being gone?"

I couldn't lie to my BFF. "Don't fool yourself. I absolutely hate the idea of having a baby around the house! My parents are no longer anything like my parents. It's like their brains have been sucked out by aliens. But I'm sick about Togo, Nova!"

My shoulders sagged under my "I don't care what I wear" navy blue T-shirt. "Where could Togo be? She's so tiny. She's so . . . all alone." My voice choked up on the last two words. I felt all alone, too, even though I was two inches from my best friend.

Nova looked at my T-shirt and jeans. "Hey, we're dressed the same today," she said. "Of course, I always wear a blue T-shirt and jeans, but we all expect something a little artsier from you, Yumi."

"I'd dress all in black all the time if I were really going to express myself," I said. "And now I have P. E. to get through. Lucky, lucky me. I am so not in the mood."

I was changing into my gym clothes while chatting with Bella De Luca. You know her, right? She's often found at her dad's yummy bakery at Mall-o-Rama after school behind the counter? Long, straight, dark hair that she's always doing something cool with? Anyway, Bella and I like to share our philosophy on clothes. Her take: fashion statement! Mine: art, the more startling the better! Anyway, the two of us could talk clothes nonstop for a decade and never run out of things to say.

Ms. K., P.E. teacher supreme, marched her teensy-tiny self into the locker room to make an announcement. Ms. K. announces; she does not speak the way the rest of us mortals do. Maybe she's trying to prove she's got good lungs from all the athletic stuff she does. Or maybe she's trying to compensate for looking an awful lot like that little blond fairy sidekick of Peter Pan.

"You're running today, so do some stretches!" she chimed authoritatively. (Ms. K. also sounds like Tinker-bell. Even though she is technically announcing, she has a bell-like chime of a voice. Kind of a handicap in a P. E. teacher.)

"Yes, ma'am," I whispered under my breath. "Running—what in the world could be more fun than that?" I whispered sarcastically.

Bella and I did some halfhearted stretches. We had something way more important to do: discussing that age-old question "To tie-dye, or not to tie-dye?" A girl's got to have her priorities.

Way too soon, we were lined up at the starting line. I started obsessing about that new baby. And how I used to have such a great family, but now my parents didn't care what I did:

1. Fall in love with a kitten—who then vanishes, leaving me heartbroken?

Sure, go ahead. Just don't bother us. We have important things to think about, like if we should put shades or curtains in the baby's room.

2. Come home late, all scratched up and muddy from searching for that kitten?

Oh, whatever, Yumi. You'll be fine. You're a grown-up now, you know.

Grr.

I was wound up tighter than a clam with lockjaw. All my muscles scrunched. I was breathing hot and heavy.

So when Ms. K. finally sang out "GO!" I was out of there like a rocket. As I pounded around the track, fragments of angry thoughts blasted through my brain: . . . no more garage sales . . . I'll never set foot in a baby store, as long as I live . . . If it's bad now, how bad is it going to be when that baby is actually born? . . . They can't expect me to be happy, it wasn't my idea . . .

Well, you get the picture. It was like my brain wasn't really connected to my legs. So when I hit the finish line and Ms. K. rang out with a loud (for her) "Yumi!!" it brought me back to earth with a bang.

"What?" I said, defensively.

Ms. K. ran over to me and actually hugged me. It weirded me out!

"Uh," I said. (Have you noticed I say that a lot? I really should remember that if I can't say anything that means something, I should keep my trap shut!)

Ms. K. started leaping about, like she was doing jumping jacks, only less organized.

I just stood there gaping at her. Then I glanced around to see who else might be taking this scene in.

The answer? Nobody.

The rest of my PE class were still running. I'd beat everyone. Huh. That couldn't be right, could it?

"You beat the school record!" Ms. K. looked like she'd just gotten the world's best birthday present, something she secretly yearned for. Kind of shocked/ ecstatic, if you follow my drift.

"Oh?" I shrugged. "Well, that's good. Right?" I was thinking things like "beginner's luck" and "I guess that's what happens when I feel ticked off."

Ms. K. hugged herself. (I've always seen that in books, but never in action. It's interesting.)

"And you're not even out of breath," she gloated.

"Yeah, well, I was breathing pretty hard before we got going," I said.

She beamed at me. I'd gone from being an insig-nificant blip in the background to her favorite person in the world, evidently.

The other kids were puffing in, one by one. Ms. K. paid them no mind.

"You and me," she said, making a little pun on my name that only I noticed. She paused and grinned again. "We're going places!"

And that's how I signed up for track. Okay, so it's totally off the wall. I mean, me at track meets? Me, talking about running shoes and shin splints and read-ing Runner's World magazine instead of art zines? Get thee to Real Life!

On the other hand, I figured track had these things going for it:

1. I could be a STAR.
2. I could legitimately get out of the house in the afternoon, both for track practice as a group and for running by myself.
3. Somehow my running had blown off some steam and lifted my spirits, making me forget about my dreadful home situation (temporarily, anyway).
4. I could look for Togo, and cover a lot of ground in a hurry.

Also, there was a possible #5, but I wasn't counting on it:

5. My parents might actually notice me again.

Chapter 11

Early spring (rainy, cold, windy, chilly) was morphing into late spring (breezy, flowery, sunny, green), and I no longer needed sweats for track practice. As I ran, I noticed yellow daffodils and pink crocuses popping up in yards. At home, I tried to lay low. I spent a lot of time IM-ing my buddies and started (hey, I know this is weird) a huge collage, which was mostly pictures of cute orange kittens like the missing-in-action love of my life.

I did get quite the satisfying reaction out of the folks when I broke the news that they were the parents of a track star. Here's how that went down.

I had daydreamed during dinner that evening, all the better to tune out the unending discussion of baby names.

My mom had actually bought four books of baby names! And she carried them with her everywhere. At any given moment, she'd blurt out a name and wait for a reaction: "Zachary? We could call him Zach."

I'd usually just shrug, like "whatever," but Dad always had an opinion. In fact, he actually searched online for names of the great and famous men of history. So, that night he was countering with "George."

Mom said, in disbelief, "George? You think that's a good baby's name?"

"It was good enough for George Washington, wasn't it?"

Yep. It was giving me lots of opportunity to roll my eyes, all righty.

I broke into this fascinating (not!) discussion. Time for my big announcement. "Guess what?"

"You like 'George'?" my dad asked hopefully.

"No. I mean, it's nothing to do with baby names. Believe it or not." This subtle sarcasm appeared to be totally wasted on my parents.

"I joined the track team!"

My dad nearly choked on his mouthful of salmon.

Mom looked at me like I had orange-striped eels slithering out of my ears.

"Excuse me?" she said. "I thought you said you'd joined the track team!"

At last I had their attention . . . would wonders never cease?

"That's right. I did." I ate a bit of broccoli, very slowly. Trying to play the audience a bit. "The thing that happened was . . ." I told them the whole story, leaving out that part about how my anger toward them fueled my stunning race to victory. Okay, so I glitzed it up a bit. I love the drama, man!

"That's amazing!" Mom said when I'd finished.

Dad beamed at me. "I can't wait to watch you race, Yu!"

"Will you come to my first official race? It's two weeks from Saturday."

"Are you kidding?" Dad said. "Your mom and I will be there! We'll be the ones with the "Go, Yu" sweatshirts and the huge posters that say things like, 'That's our girl—Yumi Suzuki—in the lead!' "

I shuddered. "Dad! You wouldn't! Promise me you won't." Secretly, of course, I thought that might be totally appropriate.

Dad looked disappointed. "I love making up those banners."

"Dad!"

"Okay. I promise," he said grudgingly.

Mom patted my arm. She looked tired. It must be rough, hauling another person around all day. And it wasn't like Mom was a teenage mother or anything. She was getting up there. Too old to be having a kid, in my opinion—no matter what those doctors said.

"That is so exciting, Yumi," she said. "You continue to surprise me, in the very best of ways."

Oh, how I felt the guilt right then. Because, in truth, I hated surprises from my folks. I wanted them to be the way they always were . . . forever and ever. Maybe that wasn't fair . . . ? Maybe I should change my ways . . . ?

Nah.

School was becoming just something to get through before I could hit track practice. In fact, life was all about track. I got my mom to buy me good running shoes and I tie-dyed some old shorts of Dad's to practice in. I learned to stretch my hamstrings and strengthen my calves. In P. E., Ms. K. pretty much excused me from volleyball and softball in order to work out on the weight machines.

Most of all, I ran. I ran at track practice. I ran on my own after I got home. Sometimes I even got up at dark o'clock in the morning in order to jog and sprint. I always watched for Togo while I ran. She was nowhere.

Nova and I were eating lunch with Rani, Wendy, and Bella one day. Wendy started talking about how she was going to redecorate her room.

Nova said, "If anyone needs their room redecorated, it's me!"

I nodded. "No offense, Nova, but your room is bad. All that pink and those teddy bear ballerinas! It's like a three-year-old lives there. I'll help you paint it anytime."

"Now, Yumi has a cool room."

This was true. But . . . however . . . on the other hand . . .

Hey, I'd absolutely, totally loved it when Mom and I last redid it. The jungle murals on the walls were especially cool, with huge vibrant flowers and animals we made up on the spot.

Mom often stopped to look around at the walls in my room and share a smile with me, kind of a "look how clever we are" grin. But, of course, she was so busy with baby things that she hadn't done that in ages.

That afternoon, when I got home and (as usual) listened to Mom blabber on about the baby moving and the baby hiccupping as long as I could stand it (all of about three minutes), I escaped to my room. I looked at the walls. They were extremely cool. But they were no longer me.

I didn't feel fun anymore. I didn't feel like the fun Yumi who had lived in that room. Besides, the gigantic cats we'd painted reminded me too sadly of Togo, even though the painted cats were colors like purple with green polka dots. Well, I didn't have to keep it this way, right? Just because Mom and I had shared the painting of it?

Hey, I was "grown up" now, right? I should have a "grown up" room. One only I had any say in. I remembered Blue and her "my room suits my mood" philosophy. Yeah. I was definitely not in a wild, happy, jungle type of mood these days.

At dinner that night, Mom drank down her glass of skim milk and announced, like she was announcing the winner at an Academy Awards ceremony: "That's my fourth!"

Which caused Dad to drop his fork, run over to the graph on the kitchen wall—the one labeled "Food Groups of the Day"—to put a star in the fourth square after "nonfat or low fat dairy serving." I rolled my eyes. Were we in preschool, or what?

Mom said, "Harvey, that was such a stroke of genius! That chart really helps me keep track of all the food groups I need each day."

Dad patted Mom's belly bump. "We want this little fella—or girl—to get all the nutrition he—or she—needs."

I shoved my plate away. Suddenly, the oily KFC fried chicken Mom had been craving (which merited a gold star in "protein"), mashed potatoes and gravy ("complex carbohydrates" and, uh—grease?), and coleslaw ("leafy greens") didn't seem as appealing as they had when I sat down.

Couldn't we ever just forget about our impending doom?

"Yumi," Mom said. "What's new with you?"

What's new with me? That she was noticing she had another child besides the one waiting to be born was what was new with me.

I shrugged. I tried to think of something to talk about—anything other than babies.

"I think I'm going to redo my room," I said flatly. This ought to get a big reaction from Mom! But, no.

She ate a bite of coleslaw, no doubt meditating on

all the vitamins the baby would be in store for. "That's nice, honey."

That's nice, honey? That's how much she cares?

Okay, then.

"I'll need some money, if that's okay."

Dad said, "Sure, Yu. Fine. Makes sense that you'd want to do some redecorating with all the fixing up we're doing on the baby's room. Speaking of which . . . Iva? Did we decide for sure on the clouds for the ceiling?"

And just like that, I was dismissed.

Okay.

Fine.

See if I cared.

And that is how I ended up with flat black-painted walls. (Hey, when I rebel, I rebel!)

All Mom said when she saw it was, "How interesting."

She asked me what kind of a bedspread I had planned. In a stroke of genius, I said, "None." That would get her goat, right? For sure.

But, no.

"It's your room," she said. "You can do what you want with it. I'll bet you sleep really well with those black-out shades on your windows."

Yep. I had my black room, with no bedspread. I had my black shades that totally eliminated every single ray of sunlight. I even bought a black rug.

It was mine. All mine.

And I hated it.

But now that I had it, what could I do?

Chapter 12

On a summery-feeling sunny Friday afternoon, as I whizzed across the finish line on the school track field, I noticed the guy who had gotten there first. He was panting and walking it off, to avoid getting cramps.

"Hey, Yu," he gasped. "You're getting better all the time!"

"Thanks, Rafe." I started walking, too, alongside him.

Rafe Anderson was simply adorable, with mile-long (fast) legs, curly blond hair, and blue eyes.

The good news: He definitely knew who I was—and was friendly.

The bad news: He was the star of the track team, which meant he was the one for me to beat in order for me to become the new star of the track team.

Wow. Talk about issues.

"Want to run some weekend?" he asked carelessly.

My heart stopped.

"Sure," I gasped. Then I wondered if he would notice I was more breathless after he asked me than I had been when I'd breezed past the finish line.

I ran like the wind—actually, more like a hurricane— all the way home from school. On the way, I wondered: Is he like, INTERESTED, in me? Does he just need a running partner? Does he think he can pick up some running tips from me?

As I opened the door, I braced myself for the "Where have you been? Why didn't you call?" discussion.

But no one answered my "Helloooo?"

I tiptoed into the house. Were they perhaps charting Mom's meals on the ever handy food groups chart?

No.

Were they doing prenatal yoga in front of the television?

No.

Were they in the nursery, angsting over whether adding a sun face to the clouds on the ceiling would make Baby Suzuki happy or scare him/her into therapy later on?

No.

Ohmygosh. My mom was on the bedroom floor, with Dad bent over her! He was doing CPR on her!

"ARE YOU ALL RIGHT?" I screamed, running toward her.

Mom popped up like a Jack-in-the-box, which is saying something when you're packing a bit of a belly. Dad whipped around. They stared at me.

"WHAT??" I shrieked. I fell to my knees. "What happened to Mom?"

I crawled over to Mom, whose mouth had fallen open.

Dad clutched his chest and said, "Yumi, what's wrong with you? You're scaring Mom to death. To say nothing of your poor old dad."

I glared at him. "Never mind me, did Mom faint?" I noticed an electronic gizmo attached to Mom with some straps. "Are they monitoring the baby? Is Mom in labor? What is that?"

Mom looked at Dad. Dad looked at Mom. They burst out laughing.

Once they started explaining, I wished I didn't have to hear it.

"Studies prove babies who listen to classical music in utero are brighter," Dad announced.

"So?"

"So," Mom said, patting her belly and adjusting the electronic device hooked to it. "This is a Uter-O-Music CD player. We've got Beethoven playing for little Munchkin."

Oh, brother.

"Uh. Okay. So, why are you on the floor?"

"Dad's trying to get it to fit just right. The speakers have to be on a certain spot."

I noticed then that Dad clutched an instruction manual in one hand.

I staggered to my feet. "Well, you scared me to death," I said. "I almost passed out when I saw you stretched out on the floor like that." Whee, I was working myself up. I sounded so accusing and so upset.

My parents looked at each other and giggled like two-year-olds.

Dad said, "Gosh. Sorry, honey. We didn't mean to scare you."

But by then Mom was laughing so hard she couldn't talk. And when that woman belly-laughed, she truly had the belly for it, believe me.

I guess it must have been sour grapes ("fruits and berries") because I just couldn't resist what I did next. I made a "food groups" chart that looked EXACTLY like the one Dad made on his computer. But I toyed with the categories. Instead of "protein" I said "poison." "Complex carbohydrates" became "Complex GARBAGohydrates." "Fruits and berries" morphed into "brutes and fairies." "Dairy" turned into "dreary."

I woke up the next morning with a big grin on my face. They'd get a kick out of it! Or, at least, they'd get angry. Somehow, they were going to notice me!

But when I went into the kitchen, there was a new "food groups" chart on the wall. Mine was gone (I couldn't find it anywhere, even in the garbage can). Dad must have printed up a new one.

I rolled my eyes, which were getting tons of exercise these days. I rolled them yet again when I read the note on the counter: "Gone to framer's to pick up ultrasound photos." Now, for those of you who don't know, doctors sometimes take photos of the baby in the uterus, to see how it's coming along. Fine and dandy. My parents, of course, took their ultrasound photos, in which you could not tell a head from a butt, to a photographer's and had them enlarged to poster size. So, they had these huge blurry weird photos—in which you still could not tell a head from a butt. Of course, they had to have these treasures framed at the best framer, who happens to be an hour away.

Yikes. That's all I could say. Good thing it was Saturday. I went back to bed and pulled the covers over my head. But it actually wasn't any darker than it was without them.

Chapter 13

Well, the cat was out of the bag (and I'm not making a joke about my poor darling lost Togo). My parents, who did not want to know the sex of the baby, came home all aglow from the framer's with three gigantic gold-framed ultrasound photos (which Dad hung by my baby photos in the living room—weird??). It turned out that another customer in the framer's shop was "admiring" (at least, according to them) Suzuki Baby's portraits along with my parents. This woman, it turned out, happened to be a radiologist. She said, "So, are you happy to be having a son?"

My dad burst into tears of joy. Or so I heard—from him. About a billion times.

"Not that I don't love my girl," he kept saying.

Sure.
Right.
Yeah.

I went over to Nova's after school on Monday, after a verrrrry long weekend of being housebound with the parents of my *(shiver)* brother. Being the good friend she is, she was happy to see me excited (well, cynically semi-excited, anyway) about doing track. But I think it made her a little sad, too.

"Are you going to have time to hang out with me anymore?" she asked. She kind of laughed when she said it, like she was joking, and of course she knew I'd have time for her. But she couldn't fool me.

"Nova! Are you kidding? You think my track shoes are going to be more important than my BFF? Come on, now!"

Nova laughed again. "Okay. Right. Good," she said, "Hey! What've you and your mom been working on lately?"

"Actually, nothing." A pang of sorrow pierced me. "We were going to get into some more metal sculpture. But being pregnant is like her job and hobby all rolled into one these days."

"Bummer. I always loved seeing your art projects." Nova pulled out her electric guitar, Roxie. She strummed a few chords.

Not to change the subject or anything, but "You know Rafe Anderson?"

Nova brightened. "Track star Rafe? Yep. Well, I don't *know* him, but I know *of* him!"

I made my voice super casual. "We may run together some weekend."

"What?!" Nova laid Roxie carefully on her awful pink bedspread. "How did that come about?"

"He asked me. Nova, I thought I'd die!"

Nova screamed in delight as I hashed over the whole conversation for her. We went over it and over it: What did his face look like when he said it? Was it like he was asking me for a date? What did it all mean?

I ran home the long way, searching for any sign of orange and white fluff. Nothing. Nada. No how. Sigh. Sigh again. Oh, well. Maybe tomorrow.

Chapter 14

L continued to do very well at track practice. I had worried that I'd have to work myself into a rage the way I'd been the first time I'd awed Ms. K. But my muscles seemed to remember that they could move lightning fast, propelling me toward the finish line like crazy. And the more I practiced and the more Ms. K. coached me, the better I became. (I'm not one for false modesty, in case you haven't noticed.)

I was doing everything right, getting ready for my big race. For once in my life, I was eating like an athlete instead of a couch potato. I was loading up on lean protein, lots of low fat dairy stuff, getting my whole grains, and of course—tons of veggies and fruit. In fact, I actually let Dad make up a chart like Mom's, all the better to keep track of my running fuel. (Although it sure looked crazy, to have two of those star-studded charts hanging on the wall. Bizarre.)

Stretching . . . a little weight lifting . . . running in the evenings . . . Yep. I was gonna knock them dead on Saturday. As I worked out, I pictured my parents' proud faces (although in my daydreams, Mom wasn't pregnant . . . hey, it was *my* fantasy!)

Saturday dawned, bright and clear. Sunny, but not hot. A perfect day to dazzle at the track.

Mom bustled around the kitchen, getting me a good breakfast: oatmeal with nuts and raisins, a bowl of strawberries, and a big mug of real (not instant) hot chocolate. Man, this was living!

Mom sat beside me as I wolfed down my yummy meal.

"Honey, we can't wait to see you speed around that track," she said. "Your dad and I are so proud."

Yep, this was the life all right. All my mom's attention focused on me. The way it *should* be. (Just kidding. Okay, not really.)

She winced and grabbed her stomach.

"Mom?"

"Oh, it's nothing. The baby's kicking up a storm. Maybe he'll be a track star like his big sister."

Yeah. Back to reality. Clunk. So much for being the

star, the only star, in Mom's life. I was just the runner-up. (So to speak!)

But I couldn't help smiling to myself as I walked to school. Just wait until Mom actually saw me run. I mean, she was going to get her socks knocked off.

Man. I was feeling *good*. I had my race ahead of me—the almighty 1600 meter run—and I'd never felt so up in my life, anticipating the way it felt when I ran. In fact, I couldn't wait to get going. The wind in my face, and under my feet—it was a sensation of flying across the earth. The best feeling in the whole world.

I stretched my hamstrings and waved at Carmen Bernstein. As usual, she had her notebook and pen out. She was either covering the track meet for the school paper or taking notes to write The Great American Teen Novel.

We lined up. I didn't feel one bit nervous. In fact, I was picturing my win at the end, after four pounding laps around the track, with my folks jumping up and down ecstatically—and how I was going to pretend I didn't enjoy thinking I was the greatest. I felt focused. I didn't even glance around to see if Rafe was watching. Lucky for him this was a girls-only event. Otherwise, he'd be toast.

The whistle blew and we were off! I could feel the power pushing through my legs, my hair floating in the air, my breath flowing easily in and out of my lungs. I had never felt so good. I flew.

I was in the state of mind where I wasn't truly conscious of anything, but I did know I was way ahead of the pack. As I passed the bleachers, I pretended they were totally full of Yumi Suzuki fans, all cheering like crazy.

I closed in on the last lap. Seeing my fans—all admiring me—would ignite me. So, as I approached the roaring bleachers the third time, I looked for them. Dad had said they'd be right in front, and they were both going to wear red shirts so I could spot them waving and cheering me on as I breezed past. Nova was going to sit with them. I'd spot her wavy red hair, for sure.

My legs didn't hesitate as I sped on, my eyes scanning the front row. I was raising my hand to give the folks a huge thumbs up. I was already grinning. I looked. Looked again.

There was Nova—jumping up and down, waving both arms like crazy. She was sitting with Bella, Wendy, and Rani. I gave them all a quick wave and grin.

But, wait. Where were Mom and Dad? I looked again—and faltered.

And that's how I came in second, in a race I should have won by a mile.

Rafe patted my shoulder as I walked by him. I couldn't even look at him.

"Yumi," Ms. K. said, advancing on me with her hands on her hips. "What happened? You had it in the bag! You were so far ahead of anyone else."

I blinked, and swallowed hard. I forced a wobbly smile. "I know, Ms. K. I lost it on that last lap. Couldn't concentrate."

She stared at me.

Oh no. This is where she was going to say, "Too bad, Yumi. I thought you'd make it in track but I can see now that I was totally wrong about you."

But all she said was, "We'll work on that together. Okay, Yumi?" She looked into my eyes. "Okay? You're not going to give up on me, right? You've got all the potential in the world."

Oh, man. I was so relieved. I hadn't even known that I cared about track all that much. I mean, it had come relatively easily to me and I'd gotten tons of praise for what I could do. But somehow it had gone deeper—gotten under my skin in a way I never could have predicted. I wanted to run, and I wanted to run as fast as I could.

"I'll try harder next time," I promised Ms. K.

She grinned fiercely and squeezed my arm. "I know you will. See you Monday after school for practice?"

"You bet."

Nova, Bella, and Rani strolled up.

"You came in second!" Rani said. "And, isn't this just your first track meet? Awesome!"

"You did great!" Bella said.

And Nova hugged me. "You are so fast," she whispered in my ear.

I felt pretty good about it, until I started walking home. Where had my parents been? Why on earth would they not show up? The more I thought about it, the madder I got. Didn't they know how important this was to me? Wasn't I important enough to bother with?

I was fuming by the time I got home. I slammed that front door as hard as I could. Then I waited to be chewed out for it (you do *not* slam the Suzukis' front door. Ever. It's a crime punishable by many stern talkings-to.)

Nothing.

I opened the door and slammed it again.

Again, nothing.

Curious.

I stalked through the dining room to the kitchen, glancing into the living room as I passed by. No parents. Not in the kitchen. Nowhere.

They were probably discussing what darling quilt to put on the darling crib in the darling baby's room.

I headed toward the back of the house, just spoiling for a fight.

There they were. Mom was sitting in the rocker in the baby's room, holding a blue teddy bear in her lap. Dad was sitting on the floor by her feet, holding his cell phone to his ear.

Mom looked up. "Hi, honey."

"Hi honey? Hi honey?" I said. Okay, kind of yelled. I put my hands on my hips. "Where were you? Because of you I didn't win. I only came in second. Because you don't care about me," I swallowed hard, "I totally lost it!"

Dad clicked off his cell phone. "Yumi! Don't talk to your mother like that! Show her some respect."

"Yeah, like you guys show me respect?"

"Yumi!" Dad stood up. "Lower your voice, please. We're sorry we missed your race. But you've got to understand." He sounded furious.

Mom said, "Now, guys . . ."

"Understand?" I said. Okay—to be perfectly honest,

I was still pretty much yelling. "You bet I understand!"

"No, you don't!" Dad thundered back.

"Harvey," Mom said.

"I'll handle this, Iva! For your information, your mom wasn't feeling so great," Dad said. "There was no way to contact you. I've just been on the phone with the doctor."

Oh.

We looked at Mom, who winced. She looked down at her belly, and then put both hands on it.

She looked up at us, and said, "Uh-oh."

Chapter 15

Z can't tell you how guilty I felt. Sure, Mom had been having problems all day, but my picking a fight had sent her over the edge. To the emergency room, in fact, where she was seen by her doctor. She had to have a bunch of tests. I sat by her bed for that long, long day, in my sweaty track clothes, wishing I were a better person and doing some mental bargaining: "Let my mom be okay and I'll do better. I promise. Please let my mom be okay."

Well, in the end she was okay. Kind of. Sort of. At least, she got to come home. The doctor said the baby looked good and that things had stopped before they got started.

The bad news? Mom had to go directly to bed, and stay in bed until the baby was born. That would probably be a couple of weeks.

Great, I thought as the doctor talked on about how she could only get up out of bed to go to the bathroom, and that was it. *Look what I've done now. Mom can't even get up, because of me. Good going, Yumi.*

After we all got home, I sat with Mom. She looked awfully pale and tired. While she napped, I made her cinnamon toast. She looked surprised to see me coming in with a tray of toast and hot chocolate.

"For me?" She smiled at me. "You've got to be the best daughter ever."

And she didn't even sound sarcastic. I had to marvel at that.

"Maybe after all this," I waved my hand toward her little hill of a stomach, "is over, you'll help me redo my room again?"

Mom chewed a bite of toast. "Are you tired of it already?"

"That black isn't nearly as cheery as I thought it was going to be."

Mom looked at me. I looked at Mom. We burst out laughing.

"Sure," she said, and she practically rubbed her hands together in anticipation. "Do you have anything in particular in mind?"

"Maybe a mural of a girl racing toward the finish line?" I said, offhandedly. The idea had been to make Mom feel better. I hadn't even truly thought of a possible fix for my dreadful room. Anything other than black would suit me just fine.

Mom's eyes sparkled. She was in her element. "Black-haired girl? Kind of small?"

"But muscular." I flexed my bicep (which you can hardly see; it's like a little cartoon ping-pong ball of a muscle).

"Right. And a red-haired girl in the stands?"

I nodded.

"Plus a very proud mom and dad, cheering their daughter on?" Mom waited until I nodded again.

My heart constricted. I remembered how scared I was at the hospital that she wouldn't be okay, and how badly I felt about starting that argument with Dad. Before I even knew what I was about to say, I blurted, "The mom could be holding a little baby boy."

Tears welled up in Mom's eyes. "Nothing would please me more," she said softly.

Chapter 16

The next two weeks were busy. I kicked it up a notch at track practice, with Ms. K.'s help. She taught me to do a self-hypnosis thing, which helped me concentrate better (not that I can swear I'll never lose my focus again, but it should improve the more I work at it).

Mom and Dad had made me promise to keep up with track. At first I wasn't so sure I should. I pictured myself taking a few weeks off in order to help Mom (my fantasy included me in a white nurse's uniform, circa 1950—cap, white tights, shoes, and all—soothing my mother's troubled brow while everyone told me I was saving the day). But Dad insisted on taking more time off from work in order to stay home with her.

"Nothing, including computers, is more important than making sure your mom is okay," he said. That's kind of touching, because computers are HUGE in Dad's life.

Mom's friends also pitched in, coming by to visit and bringing casseroles and other dishes. Some of the donated dinners were really weird (like some kind of tomato gelatin thing with shrimp suspended in it—it looked like the gory aftermath of the worst car accident you've ever seen), so on those nights we either ordered out or Dad made one of his "special ingredient" stews. The special ingredient in his stews is always the same: dill pickle juice. Yep. You heard it here. The rest of the stew can vary widely according to what we have in the fridge, but he believes the pickle juice adds "spark."

Uh, whatever.

Of course, when I was home I was spending a ton of time with Mom. Maybe I was slipping. Like, although I didn't want to talk about *that baby*, it cheered Mom up so much when I did that I'd grit my teeth and make baby chitchat with her.

I actually found myself going through some of the baby catalogs and pointing out cute little boy outfits and toys to Mom. Dad would beam like, "at last Yumi is getting with the program!" I had to ignore him to avoid getting caught in trying to prove him wrong. Mom's happiness was more important than my pride at that point, I figured.

Mom had Dad bring out my baby book, and the zillions of scrapbooks with my baby pictures, locks of hair, inked hand prints, scribbly first drawings, etc., etc. The three of us spent a lot of time going through them.

"I wonder if this little boy will look like you," Mom said.

"The most beautiful baby in the entire world," Dad added. "I certainly hope so."

The weeks went by, full of track practice, searching for Togo, little grins exchanged in passing with Rafe, chitchat with Nova, and trying to help out at home. Things were good with Mom and Dad. Life was so good, it made me wonder if it wouldn't continue. Maybe my new little brother would be so adorable I'd fall in love with him.

With my world so perfect, how could anything possibly go wrong?

Chapter 17

ad!" I said, for the fifth time. And for the fifth time, he stared past me like he was in another world. He walked into doors, burnt the toast, and let the tea kettle boil dry. As the time for Mom to have the baby approached, Dad got more and more daydreamy. Mom, from her supine position on the couch or the bed, just laughed and said, "He's in pre-new baby land. Believe me, when reality strikes, it will wear off!"

"What?" he finally said.

"Good night. I was just trying to tell you good-night, Dad."

I fell into my chilly kittenless bed and then instantly into a deep, worn-out sleep.

"Yumi!" I was dreaming about beating Rafe in a

marathon, and him rewarding me with a single red rose. "YUMI!" he kept saying urgently.

I sat up, blinking my eyes against the sudden bright light. I croaked, "What, Rafe?"

Dad said, "Wake up! It's time to go to the hospital! Get your clothes on—hurry!"

I fumbled my way into sweats and running shoes, and stumbled out to the car, where Mom smiled at me from the passenger seat.

"The big day," she said softly.

Dad actually had big drops of sweat rolling off his forehead as he drove. Mom, however, seemed calm except for the times she got very, very quiet and seemed to be listening to something only she could hear.

After the nurses quit bustling around, they let Dad and me in to sit at Mom's bedside. I cringed when I saw Mom. She didn't look like herself dressed in a weirdly cheerful (yellow rabbits, anyone?) cotton nightshirt-thing, tucked into a narrow hospital bed. I stared at the big hot-tub in the corner of the room. Who did they think was going to sit in that? I tried not to look at the monitors beeping away or to smell the weird cleaning-solution odor in the stuffy little room.

Sweat broke out on my back. My heart fluttered. I was not enjoying this. And it could only get worse. Much worse.

Dad said, "We've got to decide on a name . . . soon. Not to pressure you, Iva."

They both looked at me.

I raised both hands. "Hey, I'm not making that kind of a decision! Besides, I have absolutely no clue."

Then I tried to make a little joke: "We could call him Togo."

Dad stared at me. "Like your cat?"

"It stands for 'it's got to go'." When Dad scowled, I said, "I'm just kidding!"

"Yumi, that's not funny," he said.

Well, probably not. To tell the truth, I was starting to panic again. I mean, *here it was.* It was time. Time for the baby to come. Time for me to exit out of my role as only child and star. Sure, I'd been feeling all rosy and warm lately, but now those feelings had entirely deserted me. In fact, I felt downright cranky. I didn't want a little brother! No one had asked me how I felt about a new addition to the family.

I was relieved when the nurse gave me a piercing look and asked me to step out. But then I felt all abandoned and familyless sitting in the waiting room reading decade-old sports magazines. When would this torture ever be over? I yearned to be out running the streets, looking for that elusive ball of orange and white cat fur. And totally forgetting what was happening in the family.

A knot of dread formed in my stomach as time went on. The night nurses went home, and the day nurses started their shifts. Finally, I closed my eyes and dozed off. I woke with my dad patting my shoulder.

"He's here! We can go down to the nursery and watch them weigh him. And Mom's fine. So happy!"

He hugged me.

It was not what I expected. You know how you see those adorable dimply babies in the movies and magazine ads? Well, he wasn't like that. He was a scrawny, red, blotchy, screaming thing with a gross blob where his belly button should be. I nearly gagged when I saw it.

Dad whispered, "That's the umbilical cord. It'll fall off after a while."

Not anywhere near me, I hope.

The nurse finished wiping off stuff that I didn't even want to think about. She taped a disposable diaper on him (I had trouble even thinking of that thing as a "him," to tell you the truth), put a T-shirt on him, wrapped him in a blanket, and handed him to Dad.

Dad's eyes were all swimming with tears and emotion and stuff. "Our little Ben, Yumi."

"Ben?"

"Mom and I decided, right before he was born. Benjamin Franklin, you know. One of the greatest thinkers ever. And Mom likes Ben. She's joking it's appropriate because of all the Ben & Jerry's ice cream she's eaten lately. How do you feel about it?"

I shrugged. "Ben's fine. It really doesn't matter to me."

Dad nuzzled "Ben."

"Oh, he is just so sweet," he said in a choked voice. "You forget what it's like to hold a baby in your arms. All that promise and . . . "

Around there, I tuned out.

The rest of the day was kind of a nightmare. I had a headache. Friends of the family kept filing through the hospital with flowers and baby clothes. There was lots of "ooohing" and "aaahing" going on. I tried to be as unobtrusive as possible.

Every time my parents tried to get me to hold the baby, I gave an excuse. Finally, they said, "Well, Yumi, Ben is not nearly as fragile as he looks. But we know it can be intimidating. So, when you're ready, Ben is looking forward to being held by his big sister." Then they'd lapse into baby talk, which I worked hard to tune out.

Finally, at last, Dad drove me home. I was so relieved to be somewhere quiet and peaceful. I stretched out on my bed in my black hole—I mean, bedroom. I tried to sleep, even though it was just late afternoon. Dinnertime, in fact, although no one had mentioned the fact that I might actually need a meal.

Tears of self-pity streaked down my cheeks. Suddenly, I felt miserably chilly. Without turning my lights on (and believe me, you needed lights in order to get around in the darkness of my room, even at high noon), I stumbled into my closet and started pawing through my clothes.

Suddenly I couldn't breathe. I ran out of the closet (bumping into the doorway) and then out of the room (bashing my arm against the dresser corner). Choking, I ran through the house and into the garage. I flung myself on my bike and headed for Nova's.

Luckily, she was home. I started crying the moment I saw her.

"There, there," Nova said, patting me on the back.

"The baby's here," I sobbed. "They named him Ben."

"Oh, Yumi! That's wonderful." She patted me as I cried on. "There isn't a problem, is there? The baby's okay? Your mom is okay?"

"They're fine," I choked out. "I've never seen my parents so happy. *I've* certainly never made them this happy." I cried on for a while, while Nova made her soothing sounds. "And Nova? I don't even like him. I don't think he's cute. I don't feel anything for him. I must be a freak, not to love my new little brother!"

Nova just let me blubber on for a while. Finally, I wound down. She handed me a big wad of tissues.

Then she looked me in the eye. "Yumi, you're going to be fine," she said sternly.

I sniffled. "I . . . I am?"

"Yes. You can't expect to love him right off the bat. It'll take some time."

"You think?"

"I know. Tell me how you feel about him in two weeks. Why, if you don't love him by then—I'll let you make me over again!"

We started laughing. The one time I'd made her over had been kind of a disaster.

"Oh, I was just practicing on you before. I'm an expert now!"

Nova snorted. "Right. In your dreams."

"Well, don't bet on me ever loving . . . Ben."

Nova said, "Yeah, well. Remember when you didn't like cats? From what you said, you never believed you'd love a kitten, either."

Silly Nova. Those were obviously two completely and totally different things. But having her say that reminded me of Togo. She'd been gone for forever. Things would have been so much more bearable with her around. I started crying even harder.

Chapter 18

You wouldn't believe it. I couldn't believe it either.

Mom and Ben had been home for about a week. A very long week. It was all turning out even worse than I'd ever predicted.

The baby cried all the time. He had to have his diapers changed constantly. You would not believe what the inside of his diapers looked like. I only caught a glimpse of it once, and it was such a horror that from then on I left the room when diaper-changing time came. He also spit up all the time, which meant Mom, Dad, and the furniture smelled like baby puke.

Dad was tired, too, because he insisted on getting up with Mom all night long. He and Mom snapped at each other over the tiniest things. Sometimes the baby even woke me up at night, and I was pretty far from the action.

Everyone made a huge constant fuss over him. My Grandma Suzi Suzuki visited. Instead of hanging out with me, doing some inline skating, eating at interesting restaurants, going out to the movies, like we'd always done in the past, she sat in a rocking chair and held Ben. I never thought I'd see the day when SS acted like a real grandmother! It was a sad sight. Then she wanted to talk about Ben with me.

Boring.

Let me say it one more time: Boring.

For the first time, I didn't cry when Suzi S. left.

Dad finally tore himself away from his son and went back to work. One afternoon, I was hanging out in my bedroom (anything to avoid being around the little horror). Mom knocked on the door.

"Come in," I called.

She stepped in, still in her bathrobe from the morning (not an unusual sight after she came home with the baby). She, as always, looked totally exhausted with big bags under her eyes and stringy hair.

"Please watch Ben for me," Mom said.

Not on your life.

"I can't. I've got algebra homework." I looked around

for my backpack. I actually did have algebra to work on, although I hadn't started it yet.

"Yumi."

Why should I have to do anything at all with that baby? It's nothing to do with me.

"Yumi, please. I desperately need to take a shower. It will only take me a few minutes."

I pulled my homework out of my pack and held it up.

"Do it in my room. Ben's asleep on the bed. He just went down. I'll be out of the shower before he wakes up."

"Oh, okay."

There was Ben, sound asleep in the middle of Mom and Dad's huge bed. He looked like a raisin in the middle of a cake. I sat on the floor and flipped my book open.

I was just starting to work away at the first algebra problem when I heard the shower go on.

Hurry it up, Mom.

I could hear the baby breathing, so very quietly. I went back to my problem.

Suddenly, there was an ear-splitting wail.

What in the world could have happened? I stood up. I looked at the baby. He was screwing his face up, turning red as a valentine heart, and angry as all get out.

I went out to the hall and called, "Mom?"

She started singing this stupid old song that was in some musical she loved.

I knocked on the door and yelled, "MOM?!!!"

She sang on, oblivious. It was something about washing a man right out of her hair.

Some mother she was.

I went back to her room. Oh. I saw what the problem was. He had dropped his pacifier, which had rolled to the edge of the bed. While I watched, the binkie dropped off the bed and bounced on the carpet and under the bed's dust ruffle.

Great.

I belly-crawled to the bed and tried to look under it. It was darker than my bedroom in there. I swiped my arm back and forth. No pacifier.

I stood up and looked at the baby. He was crying his heart out. I got down on my stomach again and tried to slither under the bed. Their bed is so low, though, that a snake would have a hard time squeezing under it. There was no way.

The baby screamed harder. I took my shoe off and used it to swipe back and forth under the bed. Nothing.

I ran to the hall, the baby's scream echoing in my head. I knocked and yelled, while Mom switched to some ancient rock and roll song. Just who did she think she was? Madonna? What about her kids?

Was this what she called a quick shower? Hadn't she been in there for hours?

Back in the room, the baby was crying like his heart was broken. I stood there, helpless and hopeless. This kid was like an animal. How would I communicate with him? Which led me to remember Togo. How I'd hated her at first, but just being open to her had changed me, making me finally into a cat lover. It was that weird message that had started it all. Remember? *Talk to an animal in its own language.* Hmmm.

I looked at Ben, crying away. I cleared my throat. How to talk babyese?

"Uh," I said, feeling like a total idiot. "Bluh bluh bluh?"

Incredibly, the baby's cries seemed just a bit quieter.

"Hmm. Ubba ubba dubba? Bluh bluh."

He took a big breath to scream again.

I quickly bent over him and said, "Dadda dadda dadda. Mamamamamama."

Oh, brother. This was not going to work.

"Abba dabba?" I said.

Silence.

I looked at his face. He was quiet. Listening. Listening to me.

No, what was I thinking? He was probably just gathering his strength to scream again.

"Mamamamama?" I said, just in case. "Benben-benben?"

And then—I couldn't believe my eyes. He broke out into the biggest baby smile I'd ever seen anywhere.

I rocked back on my heels, stunned. It must be just a fluke.

He started making a little grunting sound. I got back up and leaned over him.

"Uh bah? Uh bah bah?" This baby talk stuff was coming a little more naturally to me, I noticed.

He smiled again. Then, he opened his eyes and looked straight into mine.

He looked straight into my heart.

Oh, man.

I touched his tiny palm. His hand tightened around my finger.

I was sitting in the middle of my parents' bed, leaning against the mountain of pillows, holding Ben in my arms and talking, a little bit of babyese and a little bit of grown-up stuff, interspersed with a few snatches of random song.

"What in the world?" Mom sounded as shocked as if she'd found a pack of gorillas sitting on the floor of her bedroom playing Monopoly.

"Oh," I said, blinking up at her, pulled back to reality from my little world of Ben and Yumi. "Hi, Mom. Did you have a good shower?"

She just stood there for a moment with her mouth hanging open. Not the most attractive look, I might add.

I looked down at Benny. He looked so cute, sleeping in my arms. He puckered his little lips, like he was having a dream of eating or something.

Mom sat on the edge of the bed.

Please don't make a big honking deal out of this.

She looked at us a long moment, her eyes soft.

"He woke up while you were in the shower," I said. "His pacifier rolled under your bed. I can't reach it."

"Oh," she said. "Okay. Do you want me to take him now?"

"Nah," I said. "I'm fine."

Chapter 19

So. You're looking for that happy ending, right? Well, that happens only in books, you know. And this is real life. So some things turned out happy. (I'll get to that list in a moment). Others, not so much.

On the downside, I still wished sometimes I could be an only child again. Seriously, I didn't know how good I had it until it was no longer a possibility. Also, in the not-so-perfect department, money is a lot tighter. Dad's taking less overtime work to be home with his family, and Mom hasn't quite gotten her energy together enough to create art to sell in galleries.

So, whereas before when I'd idly say, "Wouldn't it be great if I learned to snowboard?" and the ultimate snowboard would suddenly appear as a gift from my folks, that kind of thing was pretty much in the past tense. Not that I was exactly neglected or anything, as my folks pointed out.

Which takes me to my "happy ending" list. First of all, BENNY! What can I say? I'm in love with my little brother, and we get to keep him forever. Nowadays when he cries, it doesn't irritate me (except at night and a few other rare occasions). Instead, I just want to help him so he can smile his incredible grin.

Secondly, I wanted to drop track in order to spend more time with my family, but my folks talked me out of it. They think I should see where this track stuff leads me, and so far it's leading me to be FAST. So, I'm getting a kick out of actually being good at something (if I say so myself—and I do), and practicing and working on it so I can be REALLY GOOD. It's fun to beat my own record.

Another huge plus, and no one should think it's not a big deal because it's far down on my list and I'm not writing that much about it, is that Nova and I got even closer. She says she thought I never needed anyone much because my life was so perfect. Well, hello?! My life went downhill, and Nova was a person I could always go to. And she says the same about me. Okay. I'm writing more about that than I planned to.

Moving on.

The best thing is what happened very early one morning a few weeks after Ben was born. I was doing a practice run, speeding down the same street where I'd once chased the orange cat that turned out not to be Togo but Blue's Jake. This time, of course, I wasn't crawling under hedges and racing across people's yards. Blue was out in her garden, planting on her knees, so I stopped to catch my breath and say hi.

"I'm so glad to see you!" she said, jumping to her feet and dashing away from me like I was carrying the plague. Her enthusiasm and instant departure puzzled me. She ran up to her house, opened the door, and went inside.

I just stood there going "Huh?"

She came out with her cat in her arms.

What?? She wanted me to pet him? She felt like he was lonely for the sight of me?

She stood there in front of me, just grinning. Then she thrust Jake at me.

Except it wasn't Jake.

"Togo!" I screamed, clutching her to my chest. Instantly, she started her motor, purring so loudly I couldn't hear what Blue was saying at first.

"I volunteer at the Humane Society, remember?" she said. "Someone brought her in late last night. I just happened to be there. When I saw her I had a funny feeling. She does look a bit like Jake, but on the other hand I'd never seen your kitty except in photos. And she's so much older now. So, I brought her home. I was going to call you later today."

I put my face to Togo's soft fur. "Oh, thank you! Thank you! I thought she was gone forever. I just can't believe it."

Blue said, "The pleasure is entirely mine."

"But I still can't figure out how she got out. How did she get out of my room? How did she get out of the house?"

Blue touched her charm bracelet lightly. "Some things you never can find a rational explanation for. That's the way of life." She looked all daydreamy, and then she shook herself. "Well."

So I brought my kitty on home to live for the rest of her nine lives. My parents were nearly as thrilled and mystified by her disappearance and reappearance. And we were equally surprised to find a beautiful silver charm on Togo's collar. It looked like my house, engraved with one fine word: FAMILY.

When I called Nova—stuttering and barely getting the words out in my excitement—she said, "Hooray for Togo! And you've got your charm! You need to wear it on a charm bracelet like mine!" And that's what I've done.

So, that's the way this story ends. Not a perfect happy ending, but on the balance pretty good, wouldn't you say?

THE END

Wait! P.S., and stuff. I forgot to tell you why I've even got this incredible journal to write in. I picked up the mail on my way home from school one day. Among all the bills and magazines, there was a plain manila envelope mailed to me, Yumi Suzuki, at my address. The return address was blank.

I tore the envelope open, and it was this bright red leather book with a big purple star on the front, and blank pages (the very one you're reading at this very moment).

I had to call Nova! But first I decided to write down all that had happened to me in that book, as you obviously know since you've read it all by now.

THE END (for real, this time!)

EXPLORE THE MYSTERIES OF CURSTON WITH KELLACH, DRISKOLL AND MOYRA

THE SILVER SPELL

Kellach and Driskoll's mother, missing for five years, miraculously comes home. Is it a dream come true? Or is it a nightmare?

KEY TO THE GRIFFON'S LAIR

Will the Knights unlock the hidden crypt before Curston crumbles?

CURSE OF THE LOST GROVE

The Knights spend a night at the Lost Grove Inn. Can they discover the truth behind the inn's curse before it discovers them?

Ask for KNIGHTS OF THE SILVER DRAGON books at your favorite bookstore!

For ages eight to twelve

For more information visit www.mirrorstonebooks.com

MORE ADVENTURES FOR THE

FIGURE IN THE FROST

A cold snap hits Curston and a mysterious stranger holds the key to the town's survival. But first he wants something...from Moyra. Will Moyra sacrifice her secret to save the town?

DAGGER OF DOOM

When Kellach discovers a dagger of doom with his own name burned in the blade, it seems certain someone wants him dead. But who?

THE HIDDEN DRAGON

The Knights must find the silver dragon who gave their order its name. Can they make it to the dragon's lair alive?

Ask for KNIGHTS OF THE SILVER DRAGON books at your favorite bookstore!

For ages eight to twelve

For more information visit www.mirrorstonebooks.com

Two ordinary girls
Two mysterious messages
Two crazy dares

Nova Rocks!

Nova secretly dreams of being a rock star. Her mom insists she take ballet. Will a mystery message help Nova follow her own dreams without breaking her mom's heart?

Carmen Dives In

Carmen's step-sister Riley is a super cheerleader, world-class diver, and all-around perfect person. Carmen wants to hate her. But when she follows her mystery message, she discovers there may be more to Riley than meets the eye.

Do a dare, earn a charm, change your life!

Ask for Star Sisterz books at your favorite bookstore!

For more information visit www.mirrorstonebooks.com